PINK MOUNTAIN

P. H. Sparks

iUniverse, Inc.
Bloomington

Pink Mountain

iUniverse books may be ordered through booksellers or by contacting:

iUniverse
1663 Liberty Drive
Bloomington, IN 47403
www.iuniverse.com
1-800-Authors (1-800-288-4677)

Because of the dynamic nature of the Internet, any web addresses or links contained in this book may have changed since publication and may no longer be valid. The views expressed in this work are solely those of the author and do not necessarily reflect the views of the publisher, and the publisher hereby disclaims any responsibility for them.

Any people depicted in stock imagery provided by Thinkstock are models, and such images are being used for illustrative purposes only.

Certain stock imagery © Thinkstock.

ISBN: 978-1-4502-0572-6 (sc)
ISBN: 978-1-4502-0571-9 (e)

Printed in the United States of America

iUniverse rev. date: 8/14/2012

For Ron. Thank you.

CHAPTER 1

▼

Bryan Delman tried to force his attention to his paperwork, but his suit felt sticky against his thin frame, and his short-cropped black hair felt like it was on fire, making it more difficult to endure his discomfort. The sun beat down on the pavement and sidewalk, casting shimmering waves skyward like barely visible wisps of smoke, and the reflection from the nearby glass of downtown offices seemed too bright for the eyes to endure. He felt a strong hand on his shoulder, startling him and making him spill his scalding coffee on his hands.

"Damn it!" he said as he moved the paperwork so it wouldn't get coffee stains. "Allen, can't you do anything without taking the opportunity to spook me? One of these days you'll do that and I'm going to knock you on your ass!"

A thin, muscular blond man, perhaps six-foot-four, stood in front of the table in a threatening posture. A black man, perhaps six foot but stocky and powerfully built, joined him. "You know he would never miss an opportunity for that shoulder," the black man stated.

"Shut up, Jason," Bryan said as he wiped coffee from his hands. He looked up and saw the black man with his

1

arms crossed in mock defiance. He was sporting a large grin. "Now what the hell are you smiling for?"

"You'll get to enjoy a full cup of coffee someday," Jason Begin said. He and the other visitor, Allen Hayes, had been partners with Bryan for some time. "How are we doing on those proposals?" he asked as he and Allan took seats at the table.

"Not good," Bryan said. "I got a call from the client this morning. Word is they want to see all the engineering specs, and they want to change all the parameters to include all the shipping divisions, not just the high-end commissions or the ones they used to build their business, but all the shipping divisions."

"How soon do they need it?" Allen asked.

"They said they would like to see it done in three days," Bryan said.

"What?" Jason almost choked on a mouthful of coffee. "There's no way we can produce that kind of material in less than two weeks. That would mean calling people in from other projects to help us."

"Yeah, well it gets better. They want an answer in twenty-four hours or the company cuts our funding and we get pulled off the project and sent back to working only on the western divisions. That means no Pacific West commissions, and no chance at new contracts."

"What the hell happened?" Allen asked.

"Brent happened," Bryan said. "That slimy weasel sold us out and took all the materials with him to the client so he could secure the contract for himself. There might be a way to salvage this."

"How?" Jason asked. "This was supposed to be the salvage effort, and we already lost the first run. If you don't have a miracle up your sleeve, we're all going to be taking some vacation time real soon."

"Think about it, guys. The client offered more money to Brent Thoricke to design this project with a team of his own—a team the client would provide. Brent brokered the idea on our behalf, so he knows the client, but he doesn't have all the materials he needs. I think if we can give the client two years with the project and guarantee shipping with their customers for that time, they might come back."

"Not bad. Who else knows about this?" Jason asked.

"Boss man knows—but only enough to know that we have to derail Brent's buyout."

"It won't be long before he finds out the rest of the details," Allen said. "You know what kind of temper he has. Where are the rest of the specs?"

"Locked away back at the office where they're supposed to be … or they should be anyway," Bryan said.

"Brent still has access to everything we have on the West Coast. He can still rob us of control of the previous contracts, and even steal the commissions on them," Jason said.

"I can change that when I get back to the office," Bryan said. "We need to keep the records closed and clean this mess up before Brent can do more damage. If he can access our projects, then he can gain control and suspend all our contracts on the West Coast, pending fraud charges. That means we only have access to the Alaska Pipeline and our north gold mine contracts."

They finished their coffee and left the din of the coffee shop behind.

Once back at the office, they worked to gather as much material as they could. The first thing Bryan had to do was to make sure all the contact lists were still where they should be and to make sure all the information for the trade unions were still locked up. He opened his safe and found all the paperwork there, but the flash drive was gone. He searched around his computer, but there was no sign of the drive. It was labeled I.O.T.C. and it was the most important part of the project because it had all the information for the overseas trade commissions.

Bryan picked up the phone and dialed a number. "Jason, the drive is gone."

"What? Where is it?"

"I don't know, but if Brent has the drive, he doesn't need anything else to run the project. I can stop him if I have time, but I need your help in here right now."

Bryan saw a number flashing on his phone. He groaned as he picked up the receiver. "Yeah? Okay. I'll be there in a couple minutes." He hung up the receiver and started for the boardroom.

The boardroom was full; all the department heads were there, as were Jason and Allen. It seemed there was going to be an inquisition.

Richard McReady, the boss at the head of the table, directed Bryan to a seat.

"What's going on?" Bryan asked. Taking his seat between Jason and Allen, he was immediately nervous. He and Richard had never had a good working relationship, especially considering Bryan didn't hide his revulsion at Richard's greedy and talentless efforts to secure profit.

"How much of the project have you been able to salvage?" Richard asked.

"What are you talking about?" Bryan asked. "I have all the paperwork in my office, every last transaction. I can get a copy of the proposals down here if you'd like."

"Can you get me the engineering specs and the contact lists?"

"I can, but why would I want to? I have everything we need safely locked away." Bryan couldn't see where this line of questioning was going or why he should be inclined to turn over such delicate information.

When Richard leaned forward, his large frame swelled, making him appear too large for his chair. He raised his voice, causing it to have a dangerous edge. "Can you get the information I want, or not?"

"Yes, but why?"

"Because this project is no longer your concern. The client you were working for called this morning and canceled all further transactions regarding this project. They would like to have all materials turned over to them by noon tomorrow. You and your team have finished work on this project."

"What? What the hell for?" Bryan said. "Just this morning we were talking about securing this thing and getting all the specs on line to include all the customers the client asked for. Does this have anything to do with Brent Thoricke stealing the idea?"

"Yes, and he said you were the one to set this all up and collect later at the expense of the company. He claimed you were going to steal from me. He claims you are the architect of this whole mess."

"You can't believe that. You know he was trying to steal our ideas and make them his own. He and I were at each other's throats on this from the beginning. You know damn well I would not have done something so obvious."

"Still, these are serious accusations that must be investigated. There is too much here that can't be ignored. Until we get this mess sorted out, you are going to take some time off. This is not negotiable."

"I can't believe I'm hearing this." Bryan said. "You don't think I would do this to hurt the company or steal profit for myself."

"No."

"Then why are you doing this?"

"Because I think Brent somehow got your codes and used them to his best advantage. I think that is how he was able to steal your idea in the first place. That is the reason for this inquiry—and why you get two weeks off."

"What about Jason and Allen?" Bryan asked.

"What about them?" Richard said. "They are not part of—nor are they subject to—this investigation."

"Sir," Allen said, "we were part of the development of this project and have just as much stake in this as Bryan. If you intend to suspend him, then you must consider us as well. The only other acceptable alternative is to let us be part of the investigation."

"That will not happen. I want to find the truth in this without personal bias to influence the outcome." Richard leveled his gaze at Allen like a sniper zeroing in on his target. "Why are you suggesting that the three of you be subject to the same scrutiny?"

"If you are asking Bryan to turn over all his materials for the purpose of this inquiry, then you are willing to admit that Brent is willing to do whatever it takes to profit from this event—and is going to secure the information before it can be used against the company. All of us developed this project, all of us are part of this, and there is no greater share of the responsibility to be directed to any one of us. That would be the fair thing to do."

"All right," Richard said as he returned his attention to Bryan. "That means all your projects for the last year will be under strict scrutiny until we get this sorted out. I will determine what projects you and your team will work on when you return from your time off. If I find anything that does not appear the way it should, there will be questions for all of you to answer. And if I am not satisfied with the results, all of you will fall hard."

"I don't understand why you are being so abrasive, but I think we understand each other," Bryan said. He understood that Richard would not allow him to profit from this if Richard's profit margin could not be maximized. He also understood that his drive had to be located in order for the investigating team to be assured Bryan was hiding nothing. There was a chance his drive would be destroyed, but that was an acceptable risk.

"Good, then before you go, you have a decision to make," Richard said. "Should this investigation result in the finding of corporate espionage or misappropriation of company funds, are you willing to make a statement as to the misconduct of Brent Thoricke?"

Bryan sat back down, thinking carefully. He hated fencing with Richard because he could never be sure where Richard would spring a trap. "I will decide what to do and what is the best course of action for all involved when I see the evidence presented. No statement will be made until that time. Is that satisfactory?"

"Yes, I believe it is." Richard said. "This meeting is concluded."

Bryan thought he had done enough to keep his head off the chopping block, but he was still concerned about the outcome. He waited for all the board members to follow Richard out. Allen and Jason remained behind as well.

"What the hell just happened in here?" Bryan asked.

"I would say we have been given a stay of execution," Allen said. "It would seem Brent beat us to the punch and convinced the client to let him have exclusive control of the project. Now he can say we stole the idea from him. I think he means to set you up, Bryan."

"Great. If I ever catch that slimy little bastard, I'm going to snap his neck." Bryan took a deep breath. "You realize you just put yourself in the firing line. I don't know how smart that was, but thank you. What's the plan now?"

"We go on vacation." Jason said. "But I think we'll be doing our resumes when we get back."

"Well, we have time to talk about what happens next. Why don't we go out of town for a while?" Allen suggested.

"You sure that's the wisest idea?" Bryan asked.

"Why not? What can Richard do to us now?"

"Not much, I suppose. What did you have in mind?" Bryan asked.

"You ever been hunting?" Jason asked.

"Yeah, years ago, but it wasn't a good experience," Bryan said.

"Okay, if you're not comfortable with that, then we can do something else."

Bryan was rubbing his left forearm without realizing he was doing so until he saw Allen and Jason staring awkwardly down at the scar Bryan was caressing. He saw his friends' concern. He tried to smile, but saw his friends were not convinced. "I was twelve when it happened. It's a story I'll save until the right time. It's okay; let's go hunting."

"Are you sure?" Jason asked.

"Yeah, let's do it. I'll deal with Richard and Brent when I get back," Bryan said.

CHAPTER 2

▼

"Where did you have in mind to go?" Bryan asked.

"Pink Mountain," Jason said.

"Where the hell is that?" Bryan asked.

"It's up north a ways, a fair drive from the city," Jason said. "A friend said I could use his cabin when I wanted. It'll be perfect for what we need."

"How do we get there?"

"We charter a flight up to Fort St. John, and drive from there. It'll take us about five hours to get to the cabin."

"Okay, what do we need to bring?" Allen asked.

"Just a few things—a change of clothes and maybe a camera. We can get groceries when we get there," Jason said. "Most of the things we need, like the hunting gear and such, are already at the cabin. Let's worry about the rest of it later. Right now, I need to make some calls and arrange for the hotel up there for the night."

The next day, the three friends met at the park and ride. From there, they boarded a shuttle to the terminal. Soon they had their gear unloaded and were in line for the flight.

"You'll see," Jason said. "The first stop is the hotel at Mason Creek. It's so quiet and the air is so clean there, you'll forget about the noise and pollution of the city very quickly."

"I just hope the flight isn't too rough," Bryan said. He had hated flying ever since he had to compile the reports for all the West Coast airports. At the time, it was a way for the failing airlines to recoup losses and increase ticket prices to maintain a competitive level with the larger, more successful companies. The reports were supposed to enlighten engineers to the problems of congestion with regard to air traffic control and propose possible solutions to alleviate the difficulties, but the reports proved to be more unsettling than he anticipated. After that, he found it more difficult to trust anyone with situations that were beyond his immediate control.

"Don't worry; you can get something to drink on the plane," Jason said. "The flight won't take long anyway."

They touched down in Fort St. John after ninety minutes. They gathered their wits—and their luggage from the carousel—and then Jason picked up the keys for the jeep they would be using for the duration of their stay.

Bryan had not realized how tense he had been for the entire flight. Even after only one drink, he felt dizzy. He managed to get the luggage loaded, and as soon as his head hit the headrest, he was asleep. He didn't move until the others roused him. He shook his head, trying to clear some of the fuzziness he still felt, but he felt his concentration was slow to return as he busied himself with unloading the bags from the trunk.

Bryan was glad that the worst part of the trip was over, but he still had to face the trip back. He parked the jeep behind the hotel and then went inside to look for his friends. He was surprised to find them sitting with drinks already on the table. "What is this?" he asked. "You guys couldn't wait for me?"

"What would be the point?" Jason asked. "You got a head start on us on the plane. You want a drink?"

"No, I want to go to my room for a moment. Order some food." Bryan turned down the darkened hallway. He could tell this place was old, could smell it in the air and see it in the walls and old paintings stained with age and water damage. Even the thick brown carpet was showing signs of wear. The doors to each room were thick and heavy, but each doorframe had reinforced metal bracing. Even the locks were upgraded, adding to the security of each room. This suggested the hotel had experienced a time of invasions—if that was the proper term—and the changes were more to protect than to modernize for aesthetic value. Still, for all its faults, the place did have an undeniable attractiveness to it, an irresistible charm that spoke of a fascinating history waiting to be told. Bryan reached his door and quietly stepped inside.

After he finished setting out the things he would need for the night, he rejoined his friends at the bar. The room was large, and quiet, and a bit too dark for his taste. The style was English, with heavy log construction and oak accents, and some historical ornamentation on the walls. There were pictures with descriptions that told of some of the logging and mining operations in the area—even pictures of prospectors in dirt-caked coveralls panning for that yellow treasure they had traveled thousands of miles to find, or other industrial types standing by the roadside in what were now only ghost towns. Bryan took a moment to read some of the history in the pictures.

The bar also had modern amenities like pool tables and televisions tuned to the sports channels.

Bryan was curious to understand why the place wasn't busier. There were only nine patrons, including his friends at a corner table. The bartender carried himself with surprising strength, despite the appearance of a lean and tired frame and weather-beaten face.

"What can I do for you?" the bartender asked. He had salt and pepper hair and deep-set eyes, but his smile was genuine. Bryan thought that those eyes must have held secrets and stories of better days behind.

"Do you have a single malt?" Bryan asked.

"Fiddich, sir?"

"Good. Double straight please."

The bartender saw the scar on Bryan's arm but pretended not to notice. As he turned to pour the scotch, Bryan heard a voice he didn't recognize.

"You are the one."

"Excuse me, what did you just say?" Bryan asked.

The bartender turned, "I'm sorry, sir?" His look was innocent.

Bryan looked around and saw everyone in the room involved in their own affairs, as though the world outside this town didn't belong, and newcomers were an unwelcome distraction. He did see one person in the bar, wearing dark clothing, and Bryan felt fear, was wary, and felt the urge to leave the bar. The person appeared to be nursing a dark beer but was not really paying attention to anything. The only details he saw were the jeans, heavy boots, and a heavy green canvas jacket covering a very large frame. The jacket was the kind you would expect to find as a winter issue in a military outlet store. "Who's that man in the corner?" Bryan asked the bartender.

The bartender focused where Bryan had pointed. "He's a local trapper, had some trouble with the law. He just don't like newcomers around here. You'd do well to avoid him if you stay here long."

Bryan accepted the bartender's explanation but thought there was more than what was being revealed. He fought to stop the sudden wave of irrational fear from gripping his spine as he picked up his drink and joined his friends at the table. When he turned to look where the person had been sitting, the dark figure was gone. Only the beer was left behind, and Bryan was left thinking that somehow this dark figure would appear again at the worst possible moment.

"What was that about?" Jason asked.

"I'm not sure," Bryan said. He stopped to think for a moment. "It was … it's nothing." He turned to his chicken fingers and fries, but he barely chewed each mouthful as the food went down. They all sipped their drinks, letting the night slowly pass away until it was time to retire. Bryan left most of his drink on the table; in his room, the lights were left on.

The morning was more cheery, and the three friends met in the restaurant. The room was bright despite the fact that there were few windows, and the sun cast a warm glow off the dark wood and polished brass of the front counter. They each had strong coffee and light meals, and the morning conversation was kept just as light. Bryan tried not to think of the mysterious stranger.

Soon the conversation turned to the reason they were here. "So where did you have in mind to get started?" Bryan asked.

"Well, I hadn't really thought about it, but I suppose we could get started in the woods," Jason said. He was always the one to start the day with the wisecracks.

"You are such a smartass, you know that?" Bryan said. "So what are we supposed to use, big sticks and harsh language?"

"Actually, I thought we'd just scare the moose and then lure it close enough to serve it your cooking."

"That's it." Bryan held up a finger. "I'm going to tie you to a tree with big cardboard antlers stapled to your head and yell to the first stupid trapper I see, 'Hey look, a moose!'"

Allen could no longer hold back his laughter; the other two exchanged exaggerated gestures, snarls, and scowls. The waitress came over to offer what assistance she could, but she was rudely shooed away by Bryan as he and Jason started growling and snapping. The noise caught the attention of several patrons, but they dismissed the disturbance with nods and shakes of disapproval. The waitress saw the game and poured more coffee.

"I'm sorry," Allen said. "You'll have to excuse my pets. They've been housebroken only a few days."

The waitress smiled and walked away, saying nothing.

"You two apes are going to get us kicked off this damn mountain if you keep this up," Allen said.

Bryan and Jason turned to Allen and snorted. The mischief stopped for the moment, but both men had fire in their eyes as they finished their coffee. They knew the game had just begun.

With the breakfast circus completed and the mood a bit lighter, they made preparations for the day. Jason brought the gear to the front desk while Bryan drove the jeep around to the front lot. "It won't take us long to get there once we get on the road."

"Where is there?" Bryan asked.

"In the woods," Jason said.

Bryan waited until Jason's back was turned and then stuck out his tongue once Jason couldn't see.

"There had better be a damn good reason he's not saying anything," Bryan said.

"There is," Allen said. "When a hunter has a good spot to bag an animal or two, he does not reveal his secret—not even to his best friend."

Bryan turned on Allen. "You knew this and you didn't tell me. I cause a scene in the restaurant, probably scaring the hell out of everyone in there, and you just sit there grinning your face off."

"Oh, it wasn't as b—"

"Shut up!" Bryan said. "I'm not through griping yet."

Allen was trying to stifle his growing smile.

"Don't you dare smile. You know this will be a source of amusement for him for the entire trip. If you add to this, I will shoot you right here." Bryan waited and watched, but Allen could no longer hold back the chuckling. "You are writing your own epitaph, and, by Jesus, I *will* bag the first animal and stand over your sweating carcass as you clean it for me. We'll see how you laugh then, smartass."

Jason came ambling out from the hotel office. Bryan moved to intercept, but he was not fast enough to stop the next phase of the confrontation.

"Sweet water-walkin' Jesus, it gone be a hot day. We gone bags us a moosie, yups, an' thins a gone be fine. Yups, we gone have us a time, garronteed."

Jason climbed into the driver side, and waited with an exaggerated smile. Bryan clenched his jaws; his anger had reached a fever pitch. He looked at Allen. "Get in the jeep and don't say a word."

The drive started in silence—and a long time passed before Allen broke the ice. "You were rubbing that scar on your arm, but you never did say how you got it. Do you think we could hear how that happened?"

My, that was gentle, Bryan thought. He looked at his friends and saw only serious expressions. He looked out the window and took a deep breath.

"I was only twelve when it happened. I went on a hunting trip with him—mainly because he wanted to show me a world within the world we know, as he would say. We were geared up, like we are now, and we were going after deer in the Yukon somewhere near Marsh Lake. I was still learning how to use a rifle, so I didn't have confidence about what I was doing. The day was hot and we didn't see much. I was beginning to think we wouldn't see anything until my father spotted something on a far ridge and we started moving toward it.

"We hadn't been traveling very long before we started hearing wolf calls. I didn't think anything about it, but my father was nervous and insisted we move faster. He never had the chance to tell me why because the wolves attacked us in a few minutes. There was a black wolf in the pack—it was the leader, I think—but it didn't attack. My father never got a shot off before he was taken down. I tried to hit anything, and killed a smaller gray wolf first.

"When I tried to hit the black wolf, it moved so fast that I couldn't see where it went before it hit me. It bit me and ripped my arm open, but as soon as it bit me, it backed off. I didn't see what happened after that because I blacked out. I was taken to the hospital where the doctors rushed around, doing things I couldn't see and trying to make me feel more comfortable. They did lots of tests and did their best to patch my arm—and this scar is all I have to show."

Bryan raised the sleeve to show the full extent of the scar from wrist to elbow. The underside of his arm showed the discoloration where the muscle had been repaired; the tooth marks were plain to see where they had done the most damage. The top of his arm showed only where the canines had sunk in deep to grip and hold. He lowered his sleeve to cover the scar.

"The doctors said my father was lucky to get us to the hospital, but he died as a result of the attack. I was there for a long time. I remember the day they told me he was dead. I didn't know what to think at first, but I remember the doctors always talking about some virus or infection they had to watch for. When I asked what was going on, they told me that rabies had killed my father—that was why they had to watch me for so long. I always got the feeling they were lying to me about something because I never saw doctors so nervous about something curable— and because my father had died so quickly.

"When I came home from the hospital, I stayed with my uncle until I was seventeen, but I never went hunting again. The only thing I have left is the hunting knife my father gave me."

Bryan rooted through his pack to find a large wrapped bundle. He carefully unwrapped it to show the hunting knife. The blade was long and wide, black with age and warm to the touch but still razor sharp. The handle was carved and polished bone with oak and leather accents.

"My father told me this knife was very special and that if I ever went hunting I should carry this knife with me. He told me the knife could help me—or it could kill me. I never got the chance to ask him what that meant." Bryan carefully handed the knife to Allen.

Allen examined the knife. "It's got a damn fine edge to it. Any idea where it came from?"

"No, I've never seen that style before," Bryan said. "It doesn't look like much, but the blade is strong. I have used it as a utility knife, and the blade has never dulled or marred. The blade is so strong that I can't bend it. I even tried to clean it, but the blade goes back to black the next day. Not even silver tarnishes that fast."

"What do these engravings mean?" Allen pointed to the fine etching on one side of the blade. The work was smooth and flawless, and it appeared to be written in an unknown script.

"I don't know." Bryan wrapped the knife and put it away. "There were days I wanted to throw the knife away, but I always thought of what my father told me. I wanted to see if he was right."

"We're here," Jason said. He pulled into a cutaway at the side of the gravel road they had been driving on for the last thirty minutes. The road was well kept, so there was little dust thrown up as the tires slid to a stop, and there was no trail left to indicate their passing.

Bryan looked out the window and saw only trees. He knew it wouldn't be wise to ask him where or why, so he decided to let his friends lead him. The trees were tall stands of fir and sequoia, and the air smelled sweet and fresh as though there had recently been rain. The large trees reminded him of a time he wanted to forget. He forced the thought from his mind; it would not do to think of such negative possibilities. He was here to have a good time.

Allen and Bryan gathered the gear from the back of the jeep. "This seems a little too easy," Bryan said.

"You mean this spot here?" Jason asked. "I dug this out years ago. The cabin is still two hours north of here. The jeep will be fine. The only thing that will likely happen is some animal will come by and smell the fumes coming from this strange machine and bugger off back into the trees." They all gathered their packs and started off.

Bryan was enjoying the hike. The sun was warm without being uncomfortable. He watched as the landscape passed before him and marveled at the mixture of flora he had never seen. He could not see this much beautiful country close to home. The forest was bursting with noise—from the local inhabitants and the soft wind moving through the trees. Occasionally he would see a squirrel in the branches or an eagle flying in the distance, and he would know they were gaining altitude. Even the high ridge and the rocks had their own warm, welcoming light, inviting this outsider to explore.

Bryan stopped for a moment to admire the scenery around him. At one point, the ridge dropped sharply away, and he saw a crystal blue lake in the distance, and he wondered if anyone had fished the lake. Bryan felt this was a place he could call home. He wanted to explore it all, and all he saw captivated his mind, so he didn't realize the exhaustion was beginning to set in.

"Let's stop a moment. I need a sip of water," Jason said.

Bryan wouldn't have realized his thirst if Jason had not said anything, but now he couldn't dig out his canteen fast enough. He took a long swig and felt the cool water running down his throat.

"Go easy," Jason said. "You'll cramp up if you take too much water right now. Save some until you get to the cabin. You can rest then."

"I'm beginning to see why you like this country. How long have you been coming up here?" Bryan said.

"Allen has been with me on a couple trips, but I have been coming up here since I was a boy. I noticed you were looking at the lake."

"Yeah. I wondered if there were fish in there."

"Not that I know of, but we can hike down and have a look. It's a deep lake, glacier fed, so it would be too cold for anything else." Jason wiped the sweat from his brow. "There's a river down there too, but it's about half a day's hike from here."

"How far is it to the cabin?"

"Not far, about an hour."

Bryan could feel his exhaustion draining away. "I assume we'll be hunting on the far side of the ridge over there." He pointed to a spot he had been admiring earlier.

"Yes. There's an open area and an easier way to get down if you want to get to the river. The fields go on for some distance, and there are some smaller ponds we can get to. The moose tend to gather in those areas, but they can be a bit moody. Are we ready?"

Bryan was not sure he was ready to continue, but he wanted to get to the cabin to figure out what to do from there. The trail sloped downward, and the air was getting heavier. "How high are we right now?"

"Only about four thousand feet, but that's why I wanted to stop. The air gets thinner, and you can hurt yourself if you're not ready for the hike."

They made it to the cabin without incident. Bryan was surprised to see the structure was log and not plank as he had expected. The windows were boarded up, and the wood had little wear or weathering. The small cabin looked as if it would be able to stand years of harsh winters.

"How cold does it get up here?"

"Pretty cold," Jason said. "It's not uncommon for it to drop to minus fifty or sixty. I don't think even I would last long in that kind of cold." He gathered all the gear and set it on the porch. "Allen, you're cooking tonight."

"What? What did I do?" Allen asked with a hurt look.

"I am not eating Bryan's cooking on our first night here—and there are no pizza places in the area."

"Up yours," Bryan responded as he pulled the groceries out. He carried the supplies into the cabin without turning around.

"Oh, you don't get off that easy. You get to come up with a good ghost story."

"Why do I always have to come up with the story?" It was Bryan's turn to look hurt.

"Yeah, I might have a story or two." Allen winked at Bryan.

Jason turned to his friends, but his look was serious now. "It is time to enjoy what might be our last time together. You are my friends—the best friends a man could ask for. You are my family, and not even a separation of ways will sever the ties we have made. I wanted you to know that." He held out his hands, and they all grasped each other's hands. "No matter what happens."

"Sick or well—I will be there." Allen said.

"No matter the trial," Bryan said. A long moment passed as they confirmed their blood oath. The friends had done everything together for the last four years, including living each other's lives. They had shared losses and gains, triumph and disappointment.

After several minutes, the mood changed. Each man had a job to do to get the cabin ready for the week. Bryan found the rifles in the closet, and he and Jason started cleaning them as Allen got to working over the stove. The smells were becoming too distracting for Bryan to concentrate. He could smell the tomato and spices, and his mouth was beginning to water in anticipation. "What's cooking in there?" he called.

"Piss off," Allen said. "You'll find out when it's ready."

"Maybe this will help," Jason said as he retrieved a bottle of twelve-year-old scotch from the cabinet beside the hutch.

"Oh, this is a treat," Bryan said. "How long has this been here?"

"Couple of years. I brought it with me on the last hunt, but I forgot it here when I left. Seems like now would be a good time for it." Jason brought down three glasses and poured doubles for each.

After the drinks were done, they settled at the table for a hot meal of chicken and greens. Allen put a carafe of coffee on the table for those who wanted it. The conversation was kept light, centering on what to expect from the area.

After the meal, Allen brought the fireplace to life while Bryan and Jason cleaned the kitchen.

"I think I'll wait on that story," Bryan said. "It's been a long day for us, and there is still a lot to do."

The others nodded in agreement. Jason replaced the scotch in its hiding place. They all watched the fire, listening as the fire popped and hissed.

When the fire was little more than embers, Allen got up to prepare for the morning while the others locked everything down for the night.

CHAPTER 3

▼

The day was overcast but still warm. Bryan, as usual, went straight for the coffee. "Looks a bit gray out there."

"This will burn off. The one thing you can count on up here is the weather does not do what you expect," Jason said. He and Bryan wasted no time going about the tasks to be done before the morning passed. Allen started preparing the morning meal, knowing the kitchen clean up was his alone.

Before long, Bryan had a good stack of firewood piled for the next few days. This task done, he replaced his hatchet and went to lend Jason a hand. He saw the tractor Jason was working on, which seemed more like a snow cat, but it was still sturdy enough to cover any terrain. "How do we look?" he asked.

"Not bad," Jason said. "The motor has a busted fuel line, but I can fix that in no time. There is enough gas to do the job, but the radiator is dry. I need oil before the engine will turn over."

"So what does all that mean?"

"I need to go back to the jeep for supplies. The rest of it is just minor stuff, clean up and such. Feel like going for a hike?"

"That will cost us most of the day. What about Allen?"

"We can ask him if he wants to go, but I'm just going to get supplies. I'm not going into town. I don't expect to be that long anyway."

Bryan nodded and left Jason to his work. The table was almost set for breakfast.

"Allen, Jason is going back to the jeep for supplies. I said I would go with him to help out. Do you want to go along?"

"Is he going into town?" Allen asked.

"No. He is just going to get the things he needs to finish repairing the tractor, but it won't be ready before tomorrow."

"Fine. Help me with the cleaning, and I'll go. Now go wash up."

"Yes, Mother."

As the trek started, Bryan noticed the day got warmer. Remembering the caution about dehydration, he decided to save as much water as he could in case the day turned oppressive. When they reached the halfway point, Bryan took a sip of water.

"I thought once the repairs were done, we could go down to the lake to see if there is a good fishing spot." Bryan saw Allen smiling, but it wasn't the kind of smile he expected. He saw the wheels turning in Allen's mind. "Whatever you're planning, think carefully before you do," Bryan said. Seeing Allen's smile grow confirmed that Allen had some nasty prank in mind, but he was waiting for the right time.

They gathered their packs and continued on. Once they reached the jeep, Jason gathered the supplies he thought he would need. "Is there normally traffic on this road?" he asked.

"Not normally," Jason said. "Only hunters and trappers use this road, and the ranger might come down once in a while."

An old truck pulled to a stop, and a small man leaned out the window.

"Morning, you guys need a hand with something?" he asked. His fair skin showed deep weather lines on his face, and his long black hair was showing a strand or two of gray. His smile and demeanor were those of a man who spent most of his time in the wild country. Though he couldn't explain why, he felt this was a man who could be trusted. Bryan liked him immediately.

"No, we're fine, just doing some repairs at our cabin," Jason said.

"You're staying at the Walker cabin, right?" the stranger asked.

"That's right. How did you know?" Bryan asked.

"That cabin hasn't seen much use in recent years, and the only people who travel this road are the locals. Trappers these days make their camps closer to town." The stranger held his hand out the window. "Name's Lyle Perry. I work over at the ranger station. Sometimes I work for the local authorities who track the poachers that roll through this area."

Bryan accepted the offered hand, and the grip was firm and warm. He then stepped back to allow his friends to accept handshakes and make introductions. "We just came up for a bit of diversion from the city."

"So where do you guys call home base?" Lyle asked.

"Vancouver, Toronto, wherever the business takes us," Bryan said.

"How do you like the country so far?"

"I have not seen this part of the country before, and I would have forgotten how scenic and unspoiled it was until I was reminded," Bryan said.

Lyle looked at the others with approval. "He's never been here before, has he?"

"No, first-timer," Jason said.

"Then allow me to extend an invitation," Lyle said. "There is a village about three miles up the road where some local folk live, and they are having a feast to celebrate the equinox. Would you like to join us for the celebrations and enjoy our hospitality tomorrow night?"

Bryan looked at his friends and shrugged while they nodded their approval. "Why not? I'm sure it will be a good night," Allen said.

"Yes, there will be music, dancing, and lots of food," Lyle said. "You'll have a good time."

"It's settled then. We'll be there tomorrow night," Bryan said.

They said their good-byes, and the truck slowly pulled away, leaving a cloud of dust as the only sign of passing.

Jason picked up the supplies and started back down the trail with the others. The silence settled on them like a cloak, and the afternoon sun was becoming hot. The sound of the wind through the trees could be heard, but there was no other sound. Jason saw fear when he looked at Bryan. "Bryan, are you okay?" he asked.

Bryan looked up, and sweat was beading heavily on his brow. "I'm fine. Can we move faster?"

Jason nodded and picked up the pace. When they reached the halfway point, Bryan wanted to continue. "Bryan, what's going on?"

Bryan's face was white. When Jason tried to put a hand on his shoulder, Bryan yanked away and kept hiking faster down the trail. Jason and Allen nodded to each other.

Once at the cabin, Bryan dropped his pack and marched to the kitchen. A strong arm pulled him around, and Bryan spilled his coffee.

"What the hell has gotten into you?" Allen asked.

Jason blocked the escape route, so Bryan had to answer.

Bryan closed his eyes and took a deep breath. "I'm sorry. I felt something back there. I can't explain it. I felt—"

"Scared?" Jason finished.

Bryan looked at Jason. "Yeah, but it was more than that. It was like hate, but I thought I was going to throw up."

"Have you felt that before?" Jason asked.

"Yeah … when I was a boy," Bryan said.

Bryan waited for Jason to move, and then he went outside to chop more wood. He remembered the panic he had felt in the field with his father. He struggled to put the thoughts out of his mind. He tried to focus on his task, but he gave up after a few minutes, putting down the axe. Perhaps going to the party tomorrow would be best for him.

Bryan found Jason working on the tractor. "How are we doing on the repairs?" he asked.

"Almost done," Jason said. "Just have to put a few things back on."

"How long?"

"About twenty minutes."

"Good. I want to go for a walk."

"What? Why?" Jason's asked.

Allen walked in behind Bryan, and the two exchanged a look.

"Because I want to go for a walk," Bryan said.

Jason finished what he was doing, raised himself to his feet, and brushed the dirt off his legs. He shook his head as he followed Bryan and Allen down the trail.

The trails led them to the riverbank. Once the sound of rushing water could be heard, he turned to Jason.

"Why did we come up here?" Bryan asked.

Jason was surprised by the question. He opened his mouth, but no words came out.

"Why did we come up here?" Bryan repeated.

"I thought we came up here to relax. What has you so damned agitated?"

"I'm sorry. I needed to ask. This place has a feeling … something special." Bryan walked over to where the water was not moving as fast. He started to wash his arms in the cold water.

"You going to tell us why you're brooding or just wash yourself?" Jason asked. He and Allen put their packs down. Jason was digging through his pack, but it was more for show than purpose.

Bryan ignored the question. He saw that the sandbar in this section of the river made fishing impossible. He thought there might be a pool on the other side, but he couldn't tell how deep the water was or how fast the current might be. The rocks in the water were too smooth to attempt a crossing. If there was any fishing to do, it would have to be farther downstream.

Jason finally retrieved a set of gloves and subtly moved up the bank to where some larger logs had washed up. Allen walked a little way into the water.

"Are you sure that's a good idea?" Bryan asked.

"Why are you so concerned for my safety?" Allen asked.

"If you're going to ask me stupid questions, I won't be. The water is freezing—get out of there."

Allen looked at Bryan as he moved to a depth where the water rushed past his knees. "No," he said.

"Fine. Stay in there," Bryan said, washing his hands. "If you get sick, it's your own fault."

Allen walked slowly around Bryan's peripheral vision. At the last second, he sprang forward and grabbed Bryan's arm. Both men fell into the water, getting soaked to the neck. Bryan shrieked. The water was cold enough to paralyze the lungs. He struggled to get out of the water without falling back in. Allen had more trouble getting out because of the way he had landed, but he reached the shoreline with more grace than his shivering counterpart.

"What the? Why did you do that?" Bryan yelled.

"Because you weren't going to tell us what was going on—and you needed a distraction from that. Besides, you needed a bath anyway."

Jason moved to higher ground, laughing as he went, to avoid being the next target. He watched as the others scrambled to get some dry clothing.

"Laugh it up, big man. We'll see how you like it when I nail your boots to the ceiling." Bryan's shivering prevented him from saying more. He wasn't really angry—just irritated at having been so easily caught off guard. "Sorry, guys, but I was feeling down. I don't want this to be our last time together."

"I don't follow," Jason said.

"I went through things no boy should," Bryan said. "What scares me more than losing myself in this place is losing my connection to you and Allen. Something scared the hell out of me back there. I can't explain it other than to say that if it came down to a question of self-preservation, I would not pause."

"I thought we settled that," Jason said.

Bryan could see there would be no questions about actions taken. Allen smiled in agreement. Bryan was not going to be left alone.

"Thank you, guys."

Once back at the cabin, they settled in for the night and watched as dusk made its way across the sky.

CHAPTER 4

▼

The morning was bright and cool, and Bryan was the first awake to take advantage of the day. He walked behind the cabin to gather a load of firewood, but he froze as an unexpected visitor ambled around the far side of the clearing and stopped to sniff the air. Bryan watched the black bear as it moved around. He saw its breath in the morning mist, sniffing the air in search of a free meal or some delicious garbage to satisfy its great appetite. He watched as it pawed the ground, looking for something edible. Bryan remained as still as possible until the bruin lost interest in the cabin, and it moved on in search of more appetizing fare.

Bryan waited until he was sure the area was clear before moving. As he put the firewood by the fireplace, he caught the scent of bacon and cursed under his breath. "It's no wonder that creature was here," Bryan said as he walked into the kitchen.

"What are you talking about?" Allen asked.

"We just had a visit from one of the locals. I imagine it was looking for the food cooking on the grill. Do you think you could let someone know when you are going to start cooking next time?"

"Aw, hell. All you had to do was yell at it."

"Uh, yeah, thanks." Bryan poured himself a cup of coffee.

"What's your plan for the day?"

"Don't really know, but I do want to go to the party tonight. Besides, I think it might be a good idea to get to know some of the people around here."

"Why the interest?" Allen turned to face Bryan.

"I don't know," Bryan said as he looked at the trail through the open window. He thought about the man in the bar—and how familiar the stranger had felt. "There's something wrong here. I don't know. I just want to go and ask some questions."

Allen put down the plates he was preparing and poured himself a cup of coffee. "What's going on, Bryan? You've been acting squirrely for the last two days."

Bryan tried to think about the irrational fear he felt. When he thought about the strange voice, his skin grow cold—like a cold breath and a shudder pulling on his nerves. "I'm afraid of something here. I know it doesn't make any sense—"

"It doesn't have to make sense," Jason said. "If there is something you need to do here, then we are not going home until that is done. Unreserved judgment in all engagements—and nothing has changed."

"What do you think we need to bring with us?" Allen asked.

"Nothing," Bryan said.

It didn't take long for the friends to get to the village. When they arrived, Bryan saw people getting things together for the feast. Others were already playing music and dancing. The sturdy log cabins were complete with solid shutters for the harsh winters. There were no roads around the village—only at the front were Bryan and his friends stopped.

Footpaths around the village kept the area looking pleasant. There was a large area near the center where the brush had been cleared away; a large fire was already burning with what appeared to be roasts turning on the spit. Stumps had been placed around another area as seats, away from the fire where people could relax.

As soon as the truck pulled up, the welcoming committee was there to greet them. Lyle led the way up the trail with two others.

"Hey, glad you could make it. We got meat burning on the fire and hot coffee ready to go."

"Well, you did say there would be free food—couldn't pass that up," Bryan said.

Lyle turned to the two men behind him; both wore jeans and heavy denim shirts. "These are my friends. John McCauley is the local ranger for the district."

A tall man of about fifty with short brown hair stepped forward and offered his hand. He was muscular and lean. When Bryan shook his hand, he found the grip firm and warm. The man was stronger than he looked but was able to maintain a gentle manner.

"This other character is Dave Morrison. He's a local tracker and spends most of his time working with the wildlife organizations and doing population counts."

Dave shook the hands of all the newcomers. He was shorter and thinner than John—and he was younger. Dave was also bald, but as he explained it, it was necessary to keep the bugs off the scalp.

"How long have you been in this area, Dave?" Bryan asked.

"Only about three years. Normally I work out of the colleges or universities around the country, but the government sent me here after they were losing count of their game stocks."

"Why should that matter here?" Bryan asked. "I mean, when the numbers get low, the government restocks, don't they?"

"You don't understand," Dave said. "Poaching in this area is big business. Game stocks and hunting mean revenue. The bigwigs want to protect their interest in this, and they do whatever they can to curb any illegal activity. I just do the counting, but most of the trappers will help out where they can—the ones that trap legally anyway. For the trappers, it's important because this is as much a way of life as it is business. They depend on the game stocks to survive."

More people were arriving as dusk made its slow crawl into the night sky. Food and drink kept flowing, and there was no shortage of conversation. Bryan found that the atmosphere was not as he had expected. Listening to John and Dave talk about the locals brought to mind a few questions of his own.

"There was someone in the bar when I arrived here," Bryan started. He was careful not to reveal what he felt about the encounter with the stranger. "This person didn't look like someone I would expect to find in a place like this. The bartender mentioned that there might have been some legal trouble." He described the stranger to his new friends.

"I know the man you are talking about," John said. "There was some trouble. I have caught him doing some poaching, but it was always minor stuff. He works for me once in a while."

"Who is he?" Bryan asked.

"His name is Henry Claude McKenzie—and he's the best damn tracker on the mountain. I hire him to help me track other poachers—the ones who turn poaching game into big business and strip mine the whole area. I wouldn't worry about Henry. About all he could do is bore you with tales of the old man."

"The old man?" Bryan asked.

"There is an old man that lives on the other side of the mountain," Dave said. "People don't travel there because of stories that he is a magician or some damn thing, but the old man never bothers anyone. He's harmless, but it makes for good storytelling."

"It would seem the stories in these hills are many. I wish I had time to hear them," Bryan said.

"There are too many to tell," John said. "Many of the stories revolve around people who disappear on the trails and are never found. Most people chalk it up to poacher activity and never give it a second thought, but sometimes I wonder if there isn't something else going on."

"What do you mean?"

John took a deep breath. "Folktales, like Sasquatch, have a certain truth in them, but that usually means there isn't enough evidence to prove what really happened. I know it sounds confusing, but I'm just saying that not every disappearance is because of poachers. Most of the time my job is simple, but I can't afford the luxury of believing in folktales."

"There are stories I could tell of the big city, but most of them you have already heard. The corruption doesn't change color—it just changes location. The news says enough," Bryan said.

"TV shows tend to be more accurate these days, but since the corruption here isn't mainstream, no one cares," John said.

"That's not what I see here. I see people getting together, having a good time, enjoying themselves and this place," Bryan said. "It's like a return to a point in history where the deadlines didn't matter."

"A convenient illusion," John said. "Most of the people here are guests—that part is true. Some of the others are runaways or strays that got lost and couldn't find their way back. They stay near the town, working in the hotel or one of the shops in the area, or find work in the mills. When I investigate missing people, I find some here. Some are here because they don't want to be found."

A large man in a green jacket pushed through the crowd, and the image of the man made Bryan feel instant panic and rage wash over him. He fought to restrain it, but he couldn't tear his eyes away from the man—and felt the irrational urge to cause great harm.

"Who is that one?" he asked.

The man was intimidating. Perhaps six and a half feet tall, he had a thick chest and powerful arms. His black hair flowed in curls around his shoulders, and he sported a well-trimmed goatee. The large man spotted Bryan, and he started a determined approach before being intercepted. John saw Bryan's pained expression and stood up to block any further advancement.

"What do you want?" John asked.

"I want to talk to him," the man growled.

"He is my guest, and this is not going to be an opportunity for you to test yourself, Anton. Back off now."

The big man looked at John and slowly backed away. "He is not part of the village."

"Neither are you," John said. Both men stared at each other, facing off. "Find someplace else to be." When the big man refused to move, John took a step forward. "Find someplace else to be or I will call the Ministry of Indian Affairs to get them to look into your business. That will make you uncomfortable for a very long time."

That had the desired effect. The big man backed away and blended back into the crowd.

Bryan let out a slow exhale and realized he was not only sweating—he was coiled like a cobra ready to strike. "What the hell was that about?"

"I apologize for that," John said. "That brute is Anton Bender. His few friends call him 'Goat.' I would watch out for him if I were you."

Bryan shook his head. "You don't get it. That is the man I saw in the bar. I think it's time to hear one of those stories."

John nodded. "Anton is a strange case. He is full of anger because of what happened to him in the past. He still believes in the racial purity of First Nations people—and he has been behind bars for trying to prove that point. He tried to hustle three tourists in billiards. When they caught him at his game, they tried to get their money back. He killed one of them by beating him to a pulp with his pool cue in front of a dozen witnesses.

The second disappeared the next day and was never seen again, but I can't find the proof I need to pin this on Anton. It's still an open case."

"And the third guy?" Bryan asked.

"The third guy kept moving, skipping town to avoid trial. I think he saw something that scared him so bad that he'll be running for the rest of his life. Anton was locked up for four years because he bartered a deal of some kind, but he is the dangerous kind that would kill you because you are white."

"Is that all there is about him?" Bryan asked.

John looked at Bryan. "There is more to the story, but here is not safe."

He led Bryan to an old gazebo. John's voice would be overwhelmed by the band's music if anyone tried to listen to them. He pointed to an older man playing a guitar that looked as old as he did.

"You see that man? He runs everything in the village, though he is more like a mayor because of the way everything is decided by the council. He can tell you all of the things that have happened here over the years, but if you want my advice, don't trust anyone."

Bryan couldn't see what the old man could say that the ranger didn't already know. John was holding something back.

John led them back to their table. "This place is a retreat. It does not exist on any map. Everyone here has something to run away from; for some, it's the law, for others, it's from something far worse. The problem is that I have no power to do anything until I see there is something wrong. All I have are suspicions."

"What do you think is going on?" Bryan asked.

"I can't say for sure, but I think it is something terrible. Meet me tomorrow. I'll try to explain if I can."

"Where?"

"The lumberyard."

"Why there?"

"Because everyone else says the bar or coffee shop."

Both men returned to where their friends were enjoying pints of ale.

Bryan looked back at the old man with the guitar and remembered John's warning. The old man was paying attention to the activity around Bryan and his friends. Lyle soon joined the friends and ordered a drink for himself.

"Have you eaten anything?" Jason asked.

"Not yet," Bryan said. "John and I were talking about the charming character of this place."

"You should try this," Allen said. "This is the best moose meat I have ever tasted. These guys know how to cook a roast."

Before long, the music changed tempo, making the crowd more cheery. Several people had squared off a section of ground for a makeshift dance floor. Bryan watched his friends on the dance floor, but he turned down all offers to join them. He felt no inclination to advertise his inept dancing skills—until Jason pushed him up, and he found himself mingling with the rest of the crowd.

Bryan was returning to get another drink for his partner when he felt a rough push from behind. As he turned, he found himself facing a younger man—and he braced for another collision.

"Idiot! You spilled my drink." The young man wasted no time setting Bryan up for the next part of the confrontation.

Bryan raised his hands when the shorter man stepped forward. At the same time, Jason and Allen saw Anton step forward to participate in the melee, but he was stopped before getting close to the area of conflict. Anton, seeing too many behind the two friends, backed off, but he never left the scene.

"Clumsy, stupid ox!" the young man yelled. "You think you can come around here and just knock people around."

"Wait a minute. I think you know this was not intentional," Bryan said. "I would be happy to get you another drink."

"You'll do more than that. You gonna clean my shirt too? You gonna apologize or I'm gonna kick your ass!" The young man was spitting as he inched further forward, forcing Bryan back. He suddenly shot out a fist, catching Bryan on the left shoulder and forcing him to take a rough step back.

"Wait a minute, this is not necessary." Bryan was losing his patience. He was trying to keep his defenses low to avoid the next level.

"You think you're going to tell me what to do? You think you can push people around?"

The young man's fist connected with Bryan's shoulder again. When the man punched a third time, Bryan moved to block it. Bryan grabbed for the hand, but the young man was too fast, and the move was reversed. Bryan found his defensive hand paralyzed. He tried to maneuver out of the hold, but he was too slow. He felt a flash of pain and blood flowing across the back of his hand as the man bit down hard on his left pinkie.

The combat was brought to a quick halt as thunder split the air. All eyes turned to where the ranger held his service pistol in the air. John holstered his sidearm and turned to the young man. "These are guests here. What the hell is wrong with you?"

"He just—"

"Shut your mouth! You do not say who stays or goes—and you should have been more careful with your feet." He turned away and took a deep breath, then returned his icy gaze. "Party's over for you. Go home." John kept his hand on his sidearm, but the young man refused to back down. "If I start the paperwork on this, you lose your traps and go back to prison. Walk away now."

"Do as he says." The guitar player strode forward. All illusions of frailty were dispelled as he moved with surprising strength and grace. The softer eyes Bryan had seen earlier flashed with fire and showed no sign of weakness. The young man paled and, nodding his acquiescence, disappeared through the crowd.

The older man turned to Bryan and said, "I must apologize for that. The young man can be hotheaded sometimes—and his anger can be difficult to predict—but I can assure you he will be dealt with accordingly. You are welcome to stay as long as you like, of course, but you should get that hand looked at before an infection sets in."

"Come on. I have a first aid kit in the truck," John said.

Jason and Allen did not move from their guard position so no one would have the same idea as Anton.

The big man, having been disappointed in the outcome, moved off in search of more appealing distractions. His friends joined Bryan while he was getting his hand bandaged.

"You okay?" Jason asked.

"Yeah, I'll be fine." Bryan held his hand as steady as he could while John washed it in alcohol and applied a clean wrap. "Wounded pride is all. Should have seen that coming."

"No one could have seen that, Bryan. You did nothing wrong. Do you want to press charges?"

"What? No." Bryan didn't feel like wasting time on pressing charges for a misunderstanding with a stupid drunk.

"Are you sure?" John asked. "There could be medical considerations here."

"You think this guy was sick?" Allen asked.

"I don't know, but I can find out," John said. "I'll run the records I have and see what comes up. In the meantime, I suggest you take it easy for a while. You don't need stitches, but there's no point in making it worse."

"Who was that guy anyway?" Allen asked.

"His name is Daniel Loben," John said, "a local trapper. He's been here on the mountain for some time, but I think he was running from something in another province. I don't really know anything about him."

"He seems to be intimidated by the old man," Jason said.

John packed up the first aid kit. "He has good reason to be. The old man runs everything here—even the trapping. All he has to do is give the word, and I can have the authorities up here to tear this place apart. Anyone hiding here would be found—and all activities would be examined. No one here wants that kind of attention; there are some here that would prefer to stay unfound."

"That means this place would no longer be secret, and that is something a person is willing to kill for." Bryan understood the kind of chaos that would cause—and he understood why the old man ruled with such harsh justice. It was a way of keeping safe the people he felt responsible for. It was an idea Bryan didn't share, but he could admire its simplicity.

"I have to get back to the station and get some work done. Are you guys going to hang around?" John asked.

"Yeah, I haven't eaten anything yet," Bryan said. "There are some things I want to try. What else do they have planned for the evening?"

"There are a couple things going on, but there are no fireworks if that's what you're looking for," John said. "Lyle tells stories about the local landmarks; you might find that of interest. Mostly it's just people mingling and having a good time."

"It's not a good idea to hike these hills after dark. Are there cabins we can use?" Jason asked.

"Lyle has already made the arrangements. Most of the people here live in the village so you won't be an intrusion."

John climbed into his truck, and the engine rumbled to life. The three friends watched until the truck was out of sight, and then they returned to the festivities.

Bryan noticed that Lyle had beckoned the three to the central campfire. "What's going on?" he asked.

"We were just about to start with the ghost stories. This is the part I like—I get to grandstand a bit." Lyle showed the cabins to the friends as they made their way across the village grounds and back to the central fire.

"I bet Bryan could tell a good fireside tale," Allen said.

"You're a storyteller?" Lyle asked. He seemed delighted to have found a kindred spirit.

"Not really," Bryan said. He gave Allen a sour look. "Besides, I can't come up with a story spur of the moment. I need time to think about it." He looked around for the old man. "I want to talk to some people first." He watched people talking and laughing as he walked through the village. Time had not affected this place.

"There are things you would miss if you stayed."

Bryan's heart jumped, and he turned to see the old man standing behind him. "Yes. If I stayed, there would be complications."

"My name is Dario Kashan. I'm sure the ranger told you about me."

"He told me you were the leader here—a mayor of sorts."

"A temporary position, I can assure you, but one quite necessary, as you have seen. There are times when I find it difficult to turn away those who would choose to stay, but it must be done for the safety of the village."

"Why? This place could be a fresh start."

"For some, this village offers escape; for others, submission. I cannot afford to let this place become a hospital for those without emotional grounding. I don't have the time to be a counselor."

"But this place can't stay secret forever. Eventually everything gets noticed—and changes."

"True, but this is not a world where the only laws set are by those who seem motivated only by the acquisition of material things. There are no maps and no directions to this village—it does not exist—and that is what I protect. May I ask what it is you do?"

"I create Internet software for companies around the world for transportation and trade of common goods. Most of the time I sit in front of a computer."

Dario directed Bryan to a table, and they sat down. Two pints of ale were placed in front of them.

"Do you not see how it all connects? You create software that makes for easier trading of resources and commodities around the world. Territory must be destroyed to find resources and create factories to supply the demand of the consumer. The cost of that industrial production is never examined for the true value of what is lost, and the cycle must continue until saturation dictates changes in the market. You, with your computer and your software, have contributed to that—even if the cost factor is immeasurable. You are not innocent in this, nor are many of the people here, including me. If allowed to continue unchecked, eventually this place would disappear and be forgotten along with so many other beautiful and pristine places of the world. That is why this place must be kept secret."

"I guess I never considered the dark reality of what was being done. It bothers you that there is so little we can do to stop the progress, and it upsets me to think of such a cold vision of our sociological order."

"What bothers me is that there are those who choose to continue with the planned eradication, perpetuating the cycle, even at the cost to all life in the territory in question." Dario saw Bryan's grim expression. "Now you see. I'm guessing our conversation has been educational, and I apologize for destroying your illusions. This is still a celebration. I leave you to enjoy the rest of your night."

As Dario walked away, Bryan marveled at the old man's depth of character. There was a timelessness about this leader. It was as though nothing could be hidden from him; his charisma and deep conversation were too much to take in. It left Bryan feeling exhausted.

As Bryan got up, his vision became foggy, but he figured that was just the excitement of the day. He joined his friends as they talked with Lyle. He couldn't make out what they were saying; it was like listening to a foreign tongue—even though he knew English was being spoken. He reached a hand out for Jason's arm. "I think I need to lie down." His words were slurred and he became too dizzy to stand or see where he was.

Jason jumped to catch Bryan before his head hit the table in front of him. He eased Bryan to the ground. Bryan tried to focus his vision, but his eyes burned, and his sinuses felt as though he had sniffed boiling acid. He closed his eyes, and darkness took him.

CHAPTER 5

▼

When Bryan opened his eyes, he was on a bed. Allen and Jason were by his side. His head was pounding, and his eyes felt as though they had been sucked into the back of his skull.

"Where am I?" he croaked.

"You're in the cabin that was assigned to us," Allen said.

"How long have I been out?"

"About four hours."

"What happened to me?"

"It would seem someone spiked your drink. We don't yet know who or why," Jason said. "What are you thinking, Bryan? You want me to find Lyle?"

"No. He didn't do this."

"How can you be sure?"

"Because he was trying to tell me something—and he could have gotten rid of me sooner than this. Whoever did this wants me scared, not dead."

"How do you know?"

"Because otherwise I would be dead now. There's something important here, but maybe I'm not supposed to know what it is."

It was hard to think with the pain radiating through the front of his head. Bryan imagined a dwarf banging away on an anvil in the corner of his mind. With every stomach-turning pulse of pain, the hammer came down again to send another throbbing wave of pressure to the front of his brain. He tried to raise himself, but the effort was so agonizing that he settled back down. "Will someone please get me some aspirin?"

Allen went to get the pills and a glass of water. Bryan snatched them and threw them into his mouth, washing them down with a sloppy gulp.

"What's the next move?" Allen asked.

Bryan tried to think. "Well, I know John is checking things for me. The person who did this is not going to reveal himself. The only thing to do is wait." After a few minutes, Bryan could feel the pain begin to ease, and the pressure subside a bit. "Is the party still going on?"

"Yeah, but most of the people are gone now," Jason said.

"Okay, we'll head back to the cabin in the morning. Let's just get some sleep," Bryan said. He was distracted by the thought that someone could get to him so easily. Sleep did not come easily, but after several long minutes, he was calm enough to keep his eyes closed.

When Bryan opened his eyes, the sun was illuminating a floor that looked as if it had not been swept in a week. His head still throbbed, but it was easier to manage. He felt the scar on his arm, and he recalled the dream about his first hunt. It was a memory he had hoped was as distant as his childhood. He cursed every time the memory forced its way to the surface of his mind.

"You ready for lunch?" Jason asked as he handed Bryan a steaming cup of coffee.

"What time is it?" Bryan asked.

"Almost noon."

"Jesus! Why didn't you get me up sooner?"

"Because you were very restless last night—and you kept muttering something about your father. Allen and I checked on you through the night, but I figured it was best to let you get as much rest as you could. We still have a long hike to do."

"Fine, but I want to go into town to pick up some supplies before we head back."

Bryan dragged himself up and started to get dressed, but his muscles were so stiff that he had trouble bending over to tie his boots. His sore hand felt as if it was on fire, and he found it difficult to concentrate. After lunch, the cabin was cleaned, but he was not allowed to help. Every contribution was refused, and he was starting to get irritated at the thought of being helpless.

Soon they were off, and Lyle was there to see them on their way. He gave Bryan a scrap of paper with a number. "If you need anything while you're here, call anytime," Lyle said.

Bryan's first stop was a store to pick up some first aid supplies. He also wanted to see John in his office. Allen and Jason agreed to wait at the hotel.

As soon as Bryan entered the store, he was hit with the strong smell of antiseptic soaps. It made him feel as though he was back at the hospital, and he tried to dismiss the thought. He passed a trapper as he walked out the front door, and his nose wrinkled from the smell of urine and bad whiskey. Bryan kept moving, saying nothing, but he found it hard to believe any trapper would allow himself to degrade to such a state. He thought of the mean streets back home, and it made a bit of sense.

Bryan found the ranger station without much difficulty. As he walked inside, he could smell a strong mixture of sweat and dirt. He was confused by his sudden ability to smell with such precision. He told himself that there was a side effect of the drug that hadn't worn off. He stopped and took a deep breath through his nose, trying to catch every scent, not realizing he was drawing attention.

"Can I help you?"

Bryan was startled back to attention. A uniformed young lady with short blonde hair sat behind a desk, waiting for his reply. Her gaze was piercing, and she looked annoyed at the disruption.

"Uh, yeah. I was looking for John McCauley. Is he here?" Bryan tried to look apologetic, but it had little effect.

"Who's asking?" the lady asked.

"My name is Bryan Delman. I—"

She picked up the phone and punched a number. "No, sir. There is a Bryan Delman here to see you." She dropped the phone. "Take a seat." She returned to her typing.

Bryan sat quietly and waited. He found the lady to be quite surly—and decided that conversation was out of the question. A moment later, John came out to the reception area.

"Bryan, I thought we were supposed to go somewhere," John said.

"Well, I thought about it," Bryan stopped himself and looked at the receptionist. They walked into John's office, and John gently closed the door behind them. "I wanted to come down to see what you had found out. Besides, as far as anyone else is concerned, I'm here to find out about my assault charges."

"Good point," John said. "Your hungry attacker, mind the pun, does have a criminal record, but it's just for minor stuff. He's usually just in the wrong place at the wrong time. The assault on you is the most serious I have so far."

"So what's his deal?"

"He ends up with the bag of goodies when the poacher gets caught."

"He's the mule."

"Yup. Like I said, minor stuff. My search did find something though. It seems Daniel was in a camp during a rather messy raid on poachers who were going after grizzly bear, but he was cleared of any connection. It does say that there was some sort of cult in the area—something about people pioneering, living off the land. It had something to do with forest magic or some damn thing."

"Are we talking about witchcraft or some other religious bunk?"

John looked at Bryan sharply. "Remember David Koresh and the Solar Temple?"

"Touché," Bryan said.

"Thank you," John said. "I have seen a lot of things in these hills. There are stories of hunters and prospectors disappearing. I have even heard of drug addicts going into the forest to be more in tune with their environment, but they usually end up dead. I find them after the animals have gnawed on them a while."

"I don't understand. How does this all connect?"

"After the raid, anyone thought to be connected to that cult just disappeared—and so did Daniel."

"You don't think something like that is going on here, do you?"

John looked at Bryan.

"Am I in danger?"

"I don't know, but if you decide to go back to the village, I advise caution. I still don't know much about the place. I'm going to poke around some more to see what turns up. What are your plans?"

"I'll head back to the cabin for now. After that, I don't know."

"Okay, if I find there is danger of any kind, you will be the first to know."

Bryan felt lost. All he could do was wait, but he had no idea what he was waiting for. When he got to the hotel, his friends were enjoying a meal. He decided to order some chicken strips to go.

"Get what you needed?" Jason asked.

"I think so. I stopped by John's office, but he didn't have much to say. He's going to keep looking."

It was the second time that Bryan had lied to his friends, but he didn't want to involve them until he had more information and could decide the safest course of action.

"So what do we do now?" Allen asked.

"We go back to the cabin and continue with our vacation." Bryan's order came quickly, and he added a nice tip to the bill. "There's no point in worrying about a problem that may not exist. We came here to get us a moose—so let's go get us a moose."

Jason and Allen were speechless, but they followed Bryan out to the jeep.

Back at the cabin, they tried to settle into the routine. Bryan found it difficult to concentrate. He had already cleaned the rifles and moved the packs to the door, and he stopped to pull out his knife. The blade was warm to the touch. He thought of his dream as he examined every detail on the hilt and blade. There was a reason why he remembered his terrible experience, but the reason was not yet clear. He was glad to have the knife with him now.

"Hey, you okay?" Jason asked.

"Yeah, I was just thinking about one of the last things my father said to me before he died. He said, 'All things in this world have a purpose. No matter what happens, you are still human and can make decisions for good or ill.' I never knew what he meant by that." Bryan carefully rewrapped the knife and replaced it in the pack. "I know that when it comes time for me to make the decision, I will be alone. No one can help me."

Bryan left Jason standing by the door and went to his room to rest—and to think about the dream.

The morning was clear, and Bryan was happy to wake with no memory of dream or discomfort. He got dressed, started the coffee, and stepped outside to fill his lungs with cool air. After a few minutes, Jason joined him.

"Where did you want to start today?" Bryan asked.

"There's a spot on the other side of the ridge that I want to try before we hit the swamp. We might get lucky."

After the coffee was done, they checked their packs and made sure to have plenty of water. Since energy bars would be all the fuel they would need, the packs could be kept light. Jason stopped at the door. "Remember, shoot the bulls; the cows are off limits."

When the day turned hot, they removed their jackets and donned caps to keep the bugs off their sweating scalps. Jason passed the time by talking about the landmarks along the trail or pointing out signs like scratched tree stumps from a bear marking its territory. Jason's purpose in all this, however, was safety. Before long, they were entering a large clearing on the other side of the ridge.

"We'll fan out here, but stay in eye contact," Jason said. "This is one of the game trails I used to follow."

The clearing surrendered to trees on the far side, but the trees were smaller and the grass was verdant. This told Bryan that the area had been ravaged by fire within the last decade, providing the soil with a rich mixture of nutrients that would regenerate the forest. He wondered what the world had been like before fire prevention programs. What would the world have looked like when the forest was allowed to burn unchecked? The fires would burn for months, but the forest would always return to its former richness. It was a phenomenon to be admired—like a magic part of the world that was always seen in essence, but never fully understood.

Bryan looked around for the others, but he kept his eyes open for movement. He saw the occasional curious wolf, but they always kept a safe distance. It made him think of his childhood, but Bryan quickly squashed the memory and kept moving.

Past the edge of the clearing, the forest was getting thicker. As the trio moved toward the north end of the swamp, Bryan heard the sharp snap of twigs. He stopped short and looked at the others. They had all heard the noise. All three dropped to their knees and waited and watched as a large black bear moved into view from the far side of a fallen tree, ripping and scraping at the rotten wood to get at the juicy grubs inside. It was less than a hundred yards from their position. No one moved as the brute raised its head, aware of something close but not sensing the possible threat. After a long moment, it returned to its breakfast until it was satisfied that all the tasty morsels had been found before lumbering off in search of another log. Bryan knew how dangerous and aggressive black bears could be. They waited a few extra minutes to be sure the bear would not return.

Bryan took a deep breath and watched as Jason indicated a new direction to travel. It would take them closer to the western end of the swamp. The terrain was difficult to tread because of the incline, but it got easier as the trees began to thin. Jason decided it was a good time to stop to rehydrate before the sun got too high.

"We seem to be having little luck here," Jason said. "We can hang around for a bit and see if anything comes around."

"I saw the occasional wolf, but I didn't think it was going to be this sparse," Bryan said.

"Actually I thought we were doing pretty good," Jason said. "We just haven't seen what we came for. I've gone days without seeing one moose. Don't forget that they can be moody—and they don't always do what you might expect. We'll try here for a bit longer before we move further down the hill. If we don't see anything today, it's not a loss just yet."

They packed up and moved on, taking their places as they started forward. Jason led them to the western edge of the swamp—out of view of anything that could be watching from the shoreline. They moved slower, listening more than watching. It seemed hours had passed before they saw any life near the edge of the swamp—and then it was only a deer.

When the sun rose higher, Bryan started feeling surly. The sun cooked his exposed skin, making it harder to focus. The snap of twigs drew him to the edge of the swamp. He spied a large animal moving to the shoreline. He crouched and raised his rifle, watching as the animal moved with slow determination into the depths, oblivious to the intruders to its feeding ground. He lowered his rifle at the sound of snapping fingers.

"That is a cow," Jason whispered.

All three men watched with restrained appreciation as the large head dipped low in the water. When the cow rose, it shook to throw the water from its eyes. They watched until the animal moved down the shoreline in search of protein-rich plants.

No other visitors arrived at the shoreline for several minutes. The sun was beginning its slow descent to the far horizon, painting the sky with marvelous hues of pink and orange. The few clouds appeared to float toward the colorful display, as if to participate in the grand design to make the night more magical for those who cared to watch. Bryan was used to joking about colorful sunsets, but he had never seen anything like this. The colors reflected off the hillside and made the hills glow. Bryan understood why someone would name this place Pink Mountain. This trip was a chance to visit the old world as it was—as it was meant to be—and he felt free. This was a place where he would be happy to get lost.

He gathered his gear and motioned for the others to do the same. Jason and Allen nodded, and they started the long hike back to the cabin.

The darkness was almost complete when they arrived at the cabin, but it didn't take long to get the gear prepared for the next long hike.

"Are we going back to the same area tomorrow?" Bryan asked.

"I don't know yet," Jason said. "I guess we'll have to wait and see."

"While you guys are discussing the idea, I want to concentrate on something else," Allen said.

"Like what?" Bryan asked.

"Like what we are going to do for meat for the rest of the trip. We didn't bring that much with us and it won't last."

"Allen, we can worry about that later," Jason said. "That's the kind of thing that irritates me—and usually spoils the trip. There is lots of game around if we need to get meat."

"Cool the fire, you two," Bryan said, stepping between the others. He waited for the others to back down before taking his place at the table. "I am not going to worry about that until the food is gone. Besides, we can make arrangements at the hotel if we have to."

The rest of the conversation centered on where the next hike would be.

CHAPTER 6

▼

John was looking through the files on his computer screen when the phone rang.

"Yes? Oh right." It was a sheriff from the district where the messy raid had taken place. "Yes, sir, I was hoping you could tell me something about the poaching ring that was exposed in your area four years ago. I'm watching someone right now that was tracked from your area—and I'm hoping you can tell me if there is any connection."

"Of course," responded a younger man's voice. "Who was the person in question?"

"A young man named Daniel Loben. I know almost nothing about him."

"Okay, hang on a sec." There was the sound of a file cabinet slamming closed, and then a short pause. "Ah, I think I have something here. It seems he is connected to someone named Bender. According to this file, Anton Bender is one bad guy."

"That much I know. He's the one that worries me. I have no information other than the file I have here, but there's really nothing I can do with him right now."

"Do you know where he is?"

"Yeah, he's in my town. What else do you have on Loben?"

"It says he was supposed to stand trial as a witness in the poaching sting, but he disappeared and we never saw him again. He didn't come back to his residence—never even picked up his stuff."

"What about Bender?"

"He is still wanted for questioning in two other murders. He isn't mentioned anywhere else, but another name comes up: Goran Karlovic."

John looked over the information in front of him. "No, that name doesn't ring any bells for me. What's the connection?"

"I don't know yet, but I'll dig deeper and get you that information. Is there anything else I can check?"

"Yeah, there was a cult that was shut down in your area some years back. I wonder if you can have someone dig up something about what was going on."

"You think this has something to do with the poaching?"

"That's what I want to find out."

"No problem. I'll get right on it and get back in a couple days."

"Thanks again." John grabbed his coat on the way out of his office. "Laura, there's going to be a file coming in soon. Can you make sure it gets to my desk?"

The blonde ranger nodded, not looking up from her typing.

John didn't like to lie to his staff, but this situation required as different an approach as he had ever done. It demanded special confidentiality because certain facts were being brought to light, facts that might be better left in the dark.

He stopped on the porch as soon as he saw Loben's truck in the drive. John stepped cautiously as he walked toward the truck, feeling the crunch of every stone of the gravel landing under his boots.

"What do you want here, Daniel?" John asked.

"I want to talk, that's all."

"About what?"

"I want to apologize for the other night."

"It's not me you need to apologize to." John noticed Anton sitting in the passenger side of the truck. "What about him? Is he here to apologize too?"

"Uh, no. He drove me here—and he's here to make sure I make good."

A pit in John's stomach grew heavy. He moved slowly to keep Daniel and Anton clearly in his vision. "Anton is not driving you around. He doesn't have a truck. Who put you up to this?"

Daniel took a deep breath. "Dario said if I wanted to stay in the village, I had to talk to the visitors and make things right. He wants to see the visitors too."

"No. I will not allow this to become another altercation. I can go talk to the visitors and see if they want to meet, but that is all I'm willing to do right now."

"Why?"

"Because he is here." John pointed to Anton. "He has no reason to be involved unless it profits him somehow. I will not allow him to turn this into an opportunity. Go home. If the visitors want to talk, you will hear from me. Go home and wait for my call."

"All right, ranger, if that's the way it has to be."

John could tell Daniel's stress level was spiking, but he knew Daniel would not push harder. He watched the old truck rumble out of sight before moving.

Perhaps it was time to see an old friend. John stepped back inside the station.

"Laura, change of plans. I'm going to stop in town to pick up some supplies. I'll be out of town for a few days. Hold everything until I get back." He didn't wait for her response.

Within an hour, John was on the trail. He didn't like to make unnecessary long trips, but if there was anything going wrong on the mountain, the old man would know. The old man had helped John in the past, but John had to make the long and dangerous hike to get to him. It would be least a day before he would see any sign of the old man. John didn't know much about him—not even his name—but he knew the old man was a recluse with an uncanny ability to figure things out.

After John had been hiking for six hours, the day started turning gray. The light was beginning to fade, making travel dangerous. He continued until he reached a point on the ridgeline that was sheltered from the wind. He found a spot against the rock face that was easily defendable; there was enough clear space to build a sizable fire to keep the animals back.

John was setting camp when he heard a twig snap. He froze, listening for whatever visitors might be approaching, but he heard no more sounds. He continued his task, but his hearing was focused on the world around him, trying to detect what might be skulking in the darkness beyond his field of vision. When the fire was going, he cleared a strip of ground to pitch his tent. He gathered his equipment and hung his pack out of reach of curious predators.

Another snap of dry wood made John freeze. Larger animals were wary enough about fire to keep their distance, but smaller ones were not so awkward to make so much noise when they were hunting—or trying to avoid being hunted. Someone was out there.

"Someone is going to die tonight," John whispered. "If you come out now, no problems have to happen," he called out. He listened to the world, trying not to restrict his senses to any one position. He carefully unsnapped his sidearm.

A shadow moved through the trees, perhaps thirty meters distant, just beyond the limit of firelight. John's pistol was up and ready. As the shadow came into view, John saw Anton Bender. "Jesus, man, you want to get killed real fast?" John lowered his pistol. "What the hell are you doing here?"

"You got good ears. I guess I should have been more careful," Anton said in a low tone.

"I asked what you're doing here."

Anton sat cross-legged in front of the fire. "You are going to see the old man, but I can't allow that. You've been digging up old bones—and you should have stayed out of this."

"Stayed out of what? And how the hell do you know what I been doing? I have seen the old man before. What do you care if I go see him now?"

"I know you been looking around a lot more than you should. You don't need to see the old man. You could have found what you wanted without coming up here."

John knew this situation was wrong. "Did you come up here to tell me this—or is something else on your mind? And while you're at it, how the hell did you track me so easily?"

Anton sat like a stone. His emotion betrayed no motive as observed his prey. "That part was easy. I can smell your stink for a thousand yards. As to why I came here—I'm here to kill you."

"Oh, is that all?" At first, John thought Anton might be joking, but when he saw that Anton's expression remained unchanged, he knew the encounter was going to be difficult. "I didn't come up here to play games, and I think you'll find killing me will prove more difficult than you expected."

"That's fine; I prefer something that fights back."

"You seem to forget that I have the gun." The fire popped as they stared at each other over the rising flames.

"It won't make any difference," Anton said with a smile.

CHAPTER 7

▼

Bryan had not slept well. Bad dreams plagued his sleep, and he had gotten no more than two hours of rest. Since he was the first awake, he made coffee and started the morning chores. He looked out the window and saw the day was gray and wet. Remembering Jason's lectures, he grabbed the extra clothing he would need for the day. Jason's precautions were something Bryan preferred not to consider trivial.

Allen stumbled into the kitchen and said, "Couldn't sleep?"

"No, I guess it's just the excitement of the past few days." Bryan didn't turn to face his friend because he knew Allen would see the lie in Bryan's face.

"We can talk about it later if you want," Allen suggested. He went back into the kitchen to start breakfast. After a moment, the musical sounds of pots and pans banging and being set for cooking was heard. Bryan saw a steaming cup of coffee hovering beside his head. He turned to see Allen with arm outstretched. "You'll feel better when we're all tromping through the woods. The meaning of all this will come together in time."

Bryan took the coffee as a thirsty man accepts a glass of water, careful not to spill any. "Thank you," Bryan said.

Allen winked and went back to the kitchen. Bryan sipped the coffee, and then he looked at the bedrooms and smiled. He carefully pulled the slug from a shell casing and slipped the shell back into the action of his rifle. Allen turned away with raised eyebrows, pretending not to notice. With a sharp snap, the breach was closed. Bryan was careful not to make a sound as he padded to Jason's room.

"You know he won't let this go unchallenged," Allen said. He waited for the storm to follow.

"I know, but that's the fun," Bryan whispered. He slowly opened the door and stepped inside, pointing the barrel away from anything that might be damaged by the percussion. The rifle made a loud pop, and Jason was almost instantly standing on the bed, painting himself against the wall.

"Jesus Christ!" Jason screamed. "What the hell are you doing?"

"Breakfast is ready," Bryan said.

"You won't be laughing when I wrap that rifle around your neck." Jason stepped off the bed and got his clothing together. "Now get me a cup of coffee—and while you're at it, see if you can dig up some strong antipsychotics."

Bryan felt better as he poured Jason a fresh cup.

Jason stomped out and snatched the coffee from Bryan's hand, spilling a little on the old wooden floor.

"Prick," he said as he sipped.

"Ah, you're just upset because you didn't think of it first," Bryan said. Allen could no longer contain himself; he was laughing almost to tears.

"You're right," Jason said. He smiled, having enjoyed the prank because it had been the perfect opportunity.

After breakfast, they geared up and were on their way. Bryan's nose was picking up odors that had previously gone unnoticed. The smell of pine and honeysuckle uplifted him. He wondered if the rain had brought certain sensations to life because of the moisture in the air. Even if they found nothing to shoot, the day would be rewarding for the hike alone.

After they had been hiking for an hour, Jason held his hand up to stop them on the trail. About three hundred yards away, they saw the outline of a large black wolf. Bryan had ever seen a wolf move that way. The animal was sniffing the air, but it didn't seem to be hunting. The wolf glared Bryan and his friends before bounding into the trees. Bryan had to wonder if what he had seen was real or imagined.

"Do wolves move like that?" Allen asked.

"No. I have never seen a wolf do that—or move that fast," Jason said.

"I have heard of rogue wolves doing strange things, but that one looked right at me," Bryan said. Some of the old fear had returned, and he had lost the ability to move his legs. His fingers tingled around the wood of his rifle. He looked at Jason and forced his legs to react in order to keep pace.

"Let's keep moving," Jason urged. He decided to pick up the pace a bit.

After an hour, they found a spot on the ridge to set up a temporary post to rest and wait for a visitor. They were soon alerted to the sounds of movement through the underbrush. A large moose appeared through the low-lying bush. As the animal raised its head, Bryan saw a large rack, with the bowl on each side measuring close to two feet across, with some of the velvet still attached to the spires of the horn. The rack alone had to weigh close to forty pounds. The bell under the chin hung almost the length of the jaw. Bryan guessed the animal had to weigh close to a ton. He had never seen anything like it except in books, but this was more impressive. The bull busied himself rubbing the antler against a smaller tree and raking through the underbrush to try to rub some of the velvet off the horn.

Bryan crouched so as not to be seen or heard—even though the animal was more than a hundred meters away. As he shifted to a more comfortable position, slipping off his pack, he watched the animal to make sure he didn't spook it and waste his chance. He could smell the musky odor of the animal as it moved. As it moved closer, the smell intensified. The rich odor made Bryan salivate; he could almost taste the salty sweetness of the meat. He sat and enjoyed the odor for a moment, and then raised his rifle and took careful aim, picking a spot just behind the front quarter. He watched through the scope as the animal's head swayed from side to side and roughed up the underbrush to remove the last of the velvet.

Bryan's heart leapt, and his throat was dry. He felt like a young boy who had just caught his first fish, but he took a deep breath, braced for the shot, and squeezed the trigger. The rifle bucked hard against his shoulder, the crack sounded its loud report, and the animal dropped where it stood. He waited a moment to be sure there were no other visitors who would try to claim the kill, and then he ran toward the carcass. He stopped once he got to the animal, dropped his rifle, and ripped his hunting knife from his belt. He sank the blade deep into the animal's chest. He pulled the knife from the wound, licked the blade, and tasted ambrosia. He savored the taste and breathed deep the smell of the fallen beast.

Allen and Jason ran up the trail, and Bryan cleaned his knife He felt as if the prize was his alone. He felt a little guilty as he replaced the knife in its sheath, and then he cleaned his hands and face and waited for his friends.

"That was a damn fine shot!" Jason said as he puffed his way up the trail.

"Not bad at all," Allen said. "This is a bloody big animal. Will the tractor be able to haul this thing down to the cabin?"

"The tractor can handle this," Jason said as he pulled out a knife and tin cup. He ordered the others to do the same. One by one, Jason filled the cups with the leaking blood, handing out the cups in turn. "Gentlemen," he started as he raised his own cup, and the others followed his lead. "It is traditional for there to be a celebration for the one who has made his first kill. This kill belongs to Bryan. We drink to celebrate and to share the life and strength of this animal." They drank the rich, red fluid. "Now we take a moment to pay our respect to the animal that has given its life for us to have food." Jason took out a large portion of bread and cheese and placed them with reverence at the base of the tree where the moose had fallen. "An offering in return for what we take," Jason whispered, and then he started to clean up the site.

"I'll stay until you come back with the tractor," Bryan suggested.

Allen and Jason nodded and were off with the packs. Bryan knew they would be a while, but he could keep himself occupied until they returned. He set about marking the site so clean up would be easier, but he stopped to look around. He felt as though something was watching him, but there was no movement or sound that he could detect. After a moment, thinking his mind was playing tricks, he returned his attention to the carcass.

Once the site was prepared, he sat with his back to the largest tree to keep a clear view of everything around him. There was nothing to do but wait. As he listened to the forest around him, he began to see in his mind what his ears could hear. Soon he was dozing as the sounds of the forest lulled him into a calm snooze. He saw everything around him clearly, but his eyes were closed. He imagined birds hopping from branch to branch in search of the perfect nesting place or a morsel of food. He watched the shorter stands of trees bend and sway in the wind. He saw himself moving through the trees as if he had been there many times, and had called this place home for most of his life.

As he padded his way through the underbrush on his way down the ridge, he spotted an old man beside a large tree about fifty meters down the trail. The old man's clothing looked to be a mixture of leather and rough woven cloth. His skin glowed with vitality despite the deep wrinkles and leathery appearance of many years.

"Who are you?" Bryan asked as he approached. He spoke, but his mouth was closed.

"A local mountain man." The old man also spoke with a closed mouth, but his thoughts were audible.

Bryan moved to see the old man more clearly, but when he moved around a tree blocking his vision and was back on the trail, the old man was gone. He searched around the base of the tree, but there was no trace the old man had ever been there.

He was left standing in a wide forest of large conifers without knowing which direction to turn. The incline of the ridge seemed steeper, but he could see blue sky. Bryan was suddenly aware he was no longer in the forest he knew, and his throat started to swell. His head snapped from side to side as he desperately tried to find a trail to identify. He started to jog back the way he thought he had come, but the more he looked, the faster he ran, and the more lost he became. Soon the rush of wind in his ears became a rumble, and the trees became no more than a blurred curtain flowing past. He ran as hard as his legs would carry him—until his heart pounded, and his head throbbed from the blood rushing to his brain.

Bryan felt the speed of his movement, and his fear mixed with exhilaration and panic. He felt his panic driving him to find his way back or be forever lost to the world he knew, but he also felt ecstasy. He began to feel anger that he might never again see the world he loved; his rage drove him faster. The desire to kill was growing in him like an inferno that threatened to overwhelm him; his fervor made him scream, and his voice was the call of a wolf. That moment of confusion made him lose his feet, and he hit the ground.

Bryan stayed still for a moment. When he tried to pull his senses together, he raised his head and winced. He saw nothing but flashes of light as pain ripped through his brain. When his vision started to clear, his prize was still in front of him. He heard rumbling in his ears, but soon he was able to identify the rumbling as the tractor grinding up the trail. He sat up, almost passing out from dizziness, and put his hand to his forehead. "Ah, dammit!" When he pulled his hand away, he saw blood covering the palm and wrist from a gash on his forehead.

Jason and Allen rushed to his side. "Jesus, what happened?" Jason asked as he quickly retrieved a towel and soaked it to wash away as much dirt and grit as he could.

Bryan looked at the man speaking, but he did not recognize the black man in front of him. After a moment, his senses came back to him, and he knew his memory was undamaged. "I don't know," he said. "I must have dozed off and had a bad dream."

Jason carefully wiped away the blood and dirt as Allen handed him the first aid kit. "I'd say from the look of this cut, your bad dream nearly killed you. This is going to need a few stitches." Jason used some solution to wash the cut, and then he took a needle and some thread from his pack.

"Are you sure this is necessary?" Bryan asked.

"Yes," Jason said. "This is going to get cleaned up before we go anywhere. Hold still."

Bryan grunted as Jason worked the needle through his skin. After a moment, Jason fixed a gauze pad and packed up the first aid kit.

"You want to tell us what that dream was about?" Allen asked.

"Not right now," Bryan said. He forced himself to his feet, still feeling dizzy. "I want to know what tree I hit."

"Why?" Jason asked.

"Because I'm going to chop it down."

"Figures. You sure you're okay?"

"I'll be fine. Let's just get this thing back down to the cabin."

Bryan reached for the rope to tie the carcass to the back of the tractor, but it was snatched from his grasp.

"You are not doing anything right now." Allen was holding the rope and pointing one end in a threatening gesture. "You have a ride back to the cabin. The only things you are going to do are load your pack and take a seat. We'll take care of the rest."

"Allen, I'm not—" Jason blocked any access to the carcass. "Okay," Bryan said.

He backed off and started putting his pack together. He took a seat and watched his friends wrestle with the moose until it was securely tied down. It would be almost nightfall by the time they arrived back at the cabin. The next day they would strip and hang the carcass, and it would be time to cut and wrap the meat in a few days. Minus the injuries to body and pride, it had been a productive day. Bryan's last thought before he turned in was to hope he didn't dream.

When Bryan looked out the window in the morning, the ground fog was beginning to clear. He heard activity in the kitchen, and he smelled the eggs and coffee. His appetite spiked, but when he got up, his head started throbbing again.

"Morning," Jason said, holding out a cup. "How are you feeling?"

"Okay, I guess," Bryan said.

"Good. I want to change that dressing and check the stitches before you do anything."

"Will you please stop mothering me?"

"Not a hope," Jason said.

"Besides, an injury like that will get you into the hospital pretty quick," Allen said. "Consider yourself mothered for at least another day. You want to help out? You can help me with dinner."

"You sure lifting a pot or two isn't going to be too much?"

"Knock it off. You want to help or not?"

There was no humor in Allen's eyes. "Yes, I'm sorry. I would like to help with dinner."

"Thank you," Allen said and walked away.

The next day started like any other—bright, warm, and inviting. Bryan was full of energy and couldn't wait to get back outside.

Allen glared at Bryan as he poured himself a cup of coffee.

"I want to do something today."

"Like what?"

"Rock climbing. I was hoping Jason would know a good spot for that."

"A good spot for what?" Jason asked as he stepped into the kitchen.

"Rock climbing," Allen said.

Bryan glared at Allen.

"Oh, do we have extra energy this morning?" Jason said. He pointed to a chair; when Bryan sat obediently, and Jason changed the gauze. "Damn, you heal fast. This cut is almost healed. Those stitches will be ready to come out tomorrow."

"So what's the word?" Bryan asked.

"We can call Lyle. I wouldn't mind going," Jason said.

"All right. We'll go rock climbing." He and Jason could only stare at each other as Bryan went to pack up for the trip.

"He seems cagey," Allen said.

"I am not being cagey. I just want to go out," Bryan called back.

"And his hearing has improved," Jason added.

Allen shook his head and started preparing breakfast.

In an hour, they were at the village. Lyle had all their gear set out to be loaded.

"So, where are we going?" Bryan asked.

"It's a place called Nelson's Cairn. It's about five hundred feet up, but it's a good spot for those who are just starting. The climb will keep us busy for the day. Why the sudden interest in rock climbing?"

"I don't know. I just wanted to try it once before I go home."

"You're in for a treat," Lyle said.

"Can you tell us about the area?" Jason asked.

"I can, but I'd like to save that story for the fireside," Lyle said. "There is more history than some will ever know, but that is where my best stories come from."

When Lyle directed Jason to stop the vehicle, Allen and Bryan unloaded the gear as Lyle and Jason retrieved the packs.

"The rock face is only ten minutes from here," Lyle said. "We'll get started after you show me a couple things."

"Like what?" Bryan asked.

"Like you remember what I showed you. You are not going to freeze up there; it's too hard to get you down."

"Fair enough," Bryan said.

They all went through the basic training with the knots and ropes until Lyle was satisfied that they could climb at minimum risk to all. The walk was easy; by the time they reached the rock face, they were warmed up enough to start stretching for their ascent. Lyle checked all the braces and harnesses to make sure they were properly assembled and strapped in.

Being the first on the line, Bryan started up in fine style. He was enjoying the exercise—until he looked down at Jason and Allen. His excitement reached a new high. He felt free, powerful, and able to overcome anything. Jason was a bit slower, but he was still making good time. Allen followed, and Lyle went last so he could guide the others to all the handholds and hooks along the way.

"I can see why this sport has such attraction following," Bryan said.

"Don't get cocky," Lyle said. "We still have a ways to go. The climb gets more difficult from here." He took up the slack and set his rope so he could maneuver around the others. "Bryan, there's a hook a few feet above you. Set your rope and get ready for the next push. The next few minutes will be easier with the extra handholds and cracks, but the climb gets real challenging after that."

Jason and Allen nodded their readiness to push on. Bryan set his rope at the anchor point with his carabineer.

He watched as Lyle ascended, checking each harness as he moved past each climber. When he reached Bryan, he set his rope on the same anchor and switched over so he could take the lead. "How do you feel?"

"Pretty good. Ready to keep going," Bryan said. He saw that he had only climbed about a hundred feet, but he felt as though he had already scaled half the face. His muscles ached a bit, but he felt exhilarated. His muscles begged him to be worked harder. He wanted to oblige them, but he understood why Lyle had to set the pace for the rest of the climb.

Lyle saw the anticipation in Bryan's face. "Take your time. We're not setting any records here. How you boys doing down there?" He finished switching the rope from Bryan's anchor to his own.

"Good. We're ready," Jason called.

"You ready?" Lyle asked. Bryan nodded. "Okay, the handholds are smaller, but there are more anchors. Follow my lead." Lyle pushed past Bryan and made his way to a large crack in the rock face.

The climb got more difficult, but Bryan felt energized by the effort. "Hey, just a thought, how do we get back down?"

"I was wondering when you'd get around to that," Lyle said. "We have to hike down the other side, but it will take about three hours to get back down. Don't worry. We'll be fine."

"That will put us close to the end of the day." Bryan swung his rope and prepared to move from his anchor point to the large crack. He moved up easily enough. When Jason and Allen followed the same route, their efforts seemed more strained. Both men were beginning to puff a bit.

Lyle set his rope to an anchor at what was roughly the halfway point. "This is a good spot to stop for a sip of water and take in the view."

When Bryan looked behind him, he saw the valley and the river below them. He could also see their ride parked at the foot of the rock face. It was easy to see that they were thousands of feet above the valley. The air was crystal clear, and there was no limit to his vision.

"Let's keep going. We still have a ways to go," Lyle said.

The wind picked up, and it made the climb a bit cooler even as the sweat continued to build on Bryan's back, magnifying the sun. Since Jason and Allen were struggling a bit, he slowed to give them time to make necessary adjustments.

When they reached a point where the cracks in the rock face were larger, movement became easier. About fifty feet from the top, Bryan could feel the ache in his arms and fingers. He had to stop periodically to ease the tension. "You guys okay?" he called.

"Feeling a bit drained here," Jason called back. The sweat was running on his skin, and he was puffing much harder. Allen appeared to be in the same state.

"When we get to the top, we'll have a rest and something to eat before we start back down," Lyle said. "One last push and we'll be there."

Bryan pushed with the last of his strength. He found that he no longer needed to use handholds. Soon he was standing at the top and encouraging his friends to push for the last few feet. Once they had reached the crest, they turned and looked down at the challenge they had overcome. They all felt proud to have accomplished something so few had tried. After a few minutes, they gathered the gear and wrapped the ropes for easier transport.

"So, we're going to do this again tomorrow?" Jason asked.

That drew a sharp look from Allen, but Bryan stepped in before Allen could react.

"I think one rock climb per vacation is enough," Bryan said. "Jason, can you help Allen with the packs and equipment?" Jason complied to avoid a confrontation. "Bryan, can you give me a hand with the ropes?" Bryan started to gather the ropes and carabiners. "What was that about?" Lyle asked when the others were out of earshot.

"This was not exactly Allen's idea of a good time," Bryan said. "He's willing to go anywhere and try anything at least once, but he does not enjoy heights. He'll look back on this day and say he had a good time, but he won't want to do this again for some time. He did it for me."

"Ha! The image of strength of the big white man is beginning to crack," Lyle said. "Still, this is a challenge for many, and for someone dealing with acrophobia, he has taken on a great thing and overcome it. He has proven a strength of fortitude that earns him his due credit. He has earned my respect this day. You seem different though."

"What do you mean?" Bryan asked.

"Come on. You're acting different, and you smell different. Something has changed with you." Lyle examined Bryan's features more closely. "Have you had a nightmare recently?"

"No."

"You're lying. What's with the bandage on your forehead?"

"What's with all the damn questions?" Bryan dropped his ropes in a pile.

"I'm asking because I think I know what's happening to you."

Bryan grabbed another rope and started to coil it. "How can you know? It's not like I just fell off my bike."

"I can't explain, but I do understand. Let's get something to eat, and we'll talk later."

Bryan tried to figure out what Lyle meant—and how he knew what Bryan could not. He watched Lyle help the others with the equipment. He had to find some answers before he could tell his friends. If he was changing, he had to figure out what it meant for them.

Jason handed Bryan a pemmican bar. "You okay?"

Bryan looked at Lyle, and the gaze was returned with a nod and smile. "Yeah. I guess I'm just a bit tired. Maybe when we get back, we can try some of that moose meat."

"We have to wait another day before we can carve it up."

"How long has the carcass been hanging?" Lyle asked.

"Two days. It was a hell of a time getting it up," Jason said.

"I bet. You and Allen haul it?"

"Yeah. We had to use the tractor. The carcass was so heavy it damn near broke the crossbeam when the rope went taut."

"Sounds like you got yourself a real prize there. If you cut and portion some of it now, it would still be okay."

"Why don't we have some tonight then?" Bryan suggested.

All four looked at each other. "Why not?" Allen said.

"Lyle, why don't you join us tonight?" Bryan asked. "Consider it a kindness returned for sharing the hospitality at the village."

Lyle said, "I accept. I would enjoy coming to your cabin and eating your moose meat." He looked at Bryan and winked as if to acknowledge the real reason for the invitation.

Bryan grabbed the harnesses and carabineers and loaded them for the hike back. The others loaded the ropes and the rest of the equipment, and then they fell in line behind Bryan as he took the lead. The trees were larger, and the rocks seemed out of place because of their great size. It was as if some powerful hand had placed them along the sides of the trail. He guessed a landslide had shifted part of the mountain. The area seemed familiar, in relation to the dream he had, but nothing was recognizable.

They stopped halfway down for a sip of water. "This area seems more rugged than any other territory I've seen. Was it always like this?" Bryan asked.

Lyle nodded as he swallowed a sip of water. "As far as I know, it has always been like this, but there are always stories about how it came to be this way. There are legends here to tell about the formations of the mountains and rivers … as there are in any other part of the world."

After a moment, they continued on down the trail. The going was rough, but manageable. The hike was taken slowly to avoid a disastrous misstep. The late afternoon sun was beating down through the trees, and it quickly raised sweat to the skin of the hikers, making it more difficult to concentrate on the obstacles on the trail. Bryan knew they had to push on until they reached the jeep because the possibility of dehydration and collapse was as real and dangerous and being stranded in the wild after dark.

By the time they were back at the jeep, the blue sky was giving way to rich hues of red and orange. As Bryan loaded the equipment, he heard the sounds of the forest changing as well. The insects started their twilight chorus, and soon other night creatures joined the concert, creating a symphony of soothing ambience after a rigorous day on the mountain.

Back at the cabin, Lyle and Allen cleaned up while Jason and Bryan carved the roast.

"So what made you decide on rock climbing?" Jason asked.

"I don't know. I just needed to do it." Bryan thought for a moment. "It was, like, testing myself. I can't explain it clearly."

The rest of the preparation was done in silence. Bryan started to salivate as the sights and smells attacked his senses. The men dug into the roast as if they hadn't eaten in days. After the meal, they retired to the front area.

"You were going to tell me things, but earlier you were cryptic. Perhaps now would be a good time to explain."

Lyle looked at the others and back at Bryan.

"They are my family," Bryan said. "What you say to me, you say to them—or I will."

Lyle shrugged. "Okay. I notice you seem to have strength in you that you probably haven't noticed yourself. You have changed more than you know since your time at the village. Have you noticed your senses augmented? Can you feel things your friends don't seem to feel?"

The question took Bryan by surprise. He had noticed things, but he'd paid them little attention and thought it was because he was away from the city. "Why are you asking this?"

"This part of the world can affect people in different ways. You have not been to this part of the world for very long. I fear that you may have experienced something that will make it very difficult to return to the world you know."

"Again you are being cryptic," Bryan said.

"How's that bite on your hand? It's almost healed, isn't it?" Lyle asked.

Bryan looked at his hand, and he was surprised to see that it was almost healed. It didn't throb or ache. There was no bruising or discoloration. It should have taken weeks to heal what was showing in just a few days. He put a hand to his forehead, but there was no scar under the bandage. The injury was minimal compared to what he had felt earlier. "How did you know?"

"You are different from the others. There are some things you will have to figure out on your own, but trust me when I say that you will never be able to return to your life as it was."

"What are you trying to tell me?" Bryan asked. Jason and Allen remained silent.

Lyle sighed, trying to gather his thoughts. "There are forces in this world that are beyond the scope of most people because they are easily ignored in favor of what their perception of the world should be. If you don't understand it, you can deny its existence. Once a truth is discovered, innocence is lost. That's all I'm going to say for now. The rest you have to discover on your own. No more questions. Besides, you have enough to think about. I have to go."

"You can't go out there now. It's pitch black out there," Allen said.

"I can get around fine in the dark. I know these hills well enough to get home."

Bryan said, "If you feel you have to go, we won't stop you. I wish you would reconsider, but I understand why you refuse." He escorted his guest to the door and watched him disappear in the darkness.

"What are you thinking?" Jason asked.

"That tomorrow we should pack up and be on our way," Bryan said.

"Are you sure that's what you want to do?" Allen asked.

"No, but I think it's the best idea right now." Bryan slowly closed the door. "I may decide to come back to this place, but for now there is no reason for me to stay."

The others nodded their agreement.

"Okay, we'll get started first thing in the morning," Jason said. "We still have a carcass to carve up and package."

They cleaned up and turned in for the night.

CHAPTER 8

▼

The sun started its slow crawl in a cloudless sky over the ridge to bathe the valley in a golden light, and the morning mist was already dissipating. Bryan was first up, so he started getting the packs and rifles together, and then he put on a pot of water for coffee.

Jason was up next, and he got started locking down everything in the cabin and backyard after all the equipment was loaded. Allen got breakfast together, but it would be cold so there was no waste—and little clean up. While the others were busy packing, Allen devoted the rest of his energy to packaging the meat for the trip home and disposing of what couldn't be used.

By midday, the work was done.

"Are we going to come back here?" Jason asked.

"Why not? I've had good experiences here, and I think I will come back," Bryan said.

"Does this have to do with what Lyle said last night?" Allen asked.

Bryan looked at Allen. "Perhaps, but I need to figure this out on my own. You need to let me do this alone. I only know I want to come back."

"You want me to set it up?" Jason asked.

"No. When I'm ready, I'll let you know."

Jason nodded and let the matter drop. He took the lead on the trail back to the jeep, setting the pace so they wouldn't tire from the heat of the day.

Bryan could feel the air getting heavier as the heat increased; he knew there would be heavy rains before they got back to the hotel. When they got back to the jeep, the clouds were already moving in. The wind picked up, but it only served to bring up the dust and grit before the rain started. As the jeep pulled onto the main road, the rain started to fall. The rain wasn't heavy, but the clouds became darker.

"Looks like the timing was perfect," Bryan said.

When they pulled into the parking lot, Allen made sure everything was locked down before joining his friends in the hotel lobby.

Bryan's eyes brightened. "What day is this?"

"It's Friday," the clerk said. "The house band is playing if you're into music and dance. It should be a good night. Are guys staying for the weekend?"

"No, just for the night," Jason said.

After the business was concluded, they went to the restaurant to pick up some food. After they had settled in their rooms, the clouds opened and unloaded. The sound of rain on the rooftop was enough to muffle the din of the restaurant and bar, and the thunder rattled and boomed its long song.

CHAPTER 9

▼

"We should think about what we're going to do when we get back," Bryan said. "I know Richard has been looking for a way to dump me for a long time now. I think he might use this opportunity to do just that."

"So what are you thinking?" Allen asked.

"I think my time with the company is over," Bryan said. "I've been thinking about this for the past few days, but I need to ask something. Is this something you guys are willing to walk away from? Are you willing to walk away from the company and leave everything behind?"

Jason and Allen looked at each other. "What exactly are you suggesting?" Jason asked.

Bryan gathered his thoughts. "We have spent a lot of time together, worked on many projects, so we have had enough time to build up a solid base of contacts and customers. Why don't we open our own office?"

"Not a bad idea, Jason. It would take some time to set up, but I don't see any reason why we can't make it work."

"And I'm sure someone is going to say it sounded like a good idea at the time when this mess is finished."

"What does that mean?" Bryan asked.

"Only that I think we need to talk this out. We all know that Richard is not going to let this go easily. What you're proposing is going to take a hell of a lot of preparation to set up. It's going to take weeks; if you really want to do this, then let's set aside a day to work it all out."

"Okay. When?" Allen asked.

"After the meeting tomorrow," Jason said. "I want to see what Richard has to say and what we can salvage from this when it's over."

"Fair enough, after the meeting then," Bryan said.

The conversation turned to small talk and reminiscing, which was fine with Bryan. It kept his mind away from the headache he was beginning to feel from the air pressure on the plane.

"Find me," a voice said in Bryan's mind. It faded like the rustling of dry autumn leaves in the wind. It was a voice he didn't recognize; it was forceful and gentle at the same time. He looked around the plane, but most of the passengers were resting or in their own conversations. Allen and Jason seemed unaware of what Bryan was feeling. Before long, the plane began to bank, and his headache began to ease, so he closed his eyes and waited for touchdown.

Disembarking seemed much smoother because the vacation was over. All Bryan could think about was his pillow. While Allen called the office, Jason grabbed a luggage cart and arranged for a cab back to the city.

"Richard said there's a meeting in two days—at nine sharp."

"Did he say anything else?" Bryan asked.

"Just that he wants all of us there."

In the cab, Bryan tried to focus on the scenery to keep from falling asleep, but the world outside the dirty windows was a blur of shades and colors. It wasn't until they passed Children's Hospital that he realized where they were. He saw nothing more until the cab stopped, and he was shaken by Jason.

"Come on, Boy Scout, we're home," Jason said.

Bryan blinked, trying to moisten into his eyes, and stepped clumsily out of the cab. "Call me in a couple days, and we'll meet at the coffee shop before we head in," he said.

He watched the cab pull away, and then he picked up his bags and stumbled through the faded green hallway. His apartment building was called Heritage, but Bryan figured that was just so someone could charge more rent. His apartment was spacious, but he had few furnishings and didn't see the need to add more as he was never home for very long. The rooms were kept dark so he could sleep at any time. He dropped his bags by the washroom, and he flopped on an old couch he had managed to hang onto since college. He slept for seventeen hours.

When Bryan woke, he was immobile. As he pushed himself to an erect position, his neck and back cracked and popped audibly. He felt a flash of pain before he began to loosen up. A hot shower helped a bit, but he still felt the fatigue of the past few days. He noticed how bad his apartment smelled. He didn't think it looked messy, but he was probably a poor judge of cleaning considering he ate out most of the time. He thought about opening the window, but it didn't seem appropriate to replace stale air with polluted city air.

Soon he was dressed and out the door. On his way down the street, he noticed a dark Malibu parked a little way up the street. He didn't think much of it at the time because there was always a crime of some kind or other going on in the area. As he passed the car, he felt wary. Once he passed the car, he paid it no more attention.

Bryan walked with an aimless gait, but then he stopped and turned as if directed—without knowing exactly why. He was looking at the front of a store he didn't remember ever being there. The old structure's façade was in need of repairs and a good coat of paint. The wood trim around the door was badly cracked and bleached from years of exposure. The windows were covered in a blanket of dust, and the cracks in the sill were caked with dirt. There were no display signs or merchandise in the windows—only a faded welcome sign taped in place. As he walked through the door, Bryan could smell years of dust, dry rot, and aged oak. They made him think of the antique shops he saw on TV. The shelves held old books, pots and pans, pewter candleholders, and just about every other sort of junk one would expect to find at a roadside secondhand store.

"Can I help you with something?" a dry, old voice said. The sound emanated from every corner of the room.

"Uh, yeah," Bryan stammered as he searched for the source of the voice. "I was hoping you could have a look at something."

He searched for the source of the voice without success. As he turned back to the counter, an old man stood there as if he had just blinked into existence. This startled Bryan a bit, and he found himself staring into the wrinkled face, rooted to the spot with fascination at what seemed impossible. His host was almost too pale, but Bryan guessed the origin of this man would have been Mediterranean.

"You said you had something for me to look at." The old man's sharp words snapped Bryan's attention back to the here and now.

"Oh, yeah, sorry." Bryan pulled out his hunting knife and unwrapped it.

The old man brought his glasses down to rest tightly on the bridge of his nose. He grabbed the knife as though it was no more than a common trinket, turning the blade over in his hands and rubbing the blade with his thumbs.

"Where did you get this knife?" the old man asked as he redirected his vision to look at Bryan with cold, unyielding eyes.

"My father gave it to me when I was very young."

"Where is he … your father?" The iron gaze never shifted focus.

"He's dead."

"Shame." The old man returned his attention to the knife. He said the word as though it was the expected response to one who had lost family, but there was no detectable emotion in his voice. "This knife is old. The markings on the blade are in a language I have never seen before. One thing is certain: if you were given this knife, then you were meant to have it for a purpose not yet revealed. The blade is a mix of steel and silver, but the strength and quality in the crafting is close to impossible to forge by today's standards. However it was done, the blade is almost unbreakable. The craftsmanship is of the finest quality I have seen for the time it was made." The old man put the knife back in the cloth and wrapped it tightly.

"What do you mean I was meant to have it?" Bryan asked.

The old man looked at Bryan with haunting eyes. "This is no hunting knife. It was crafted to kill something else, but I'm not sure you want to hear the story."

"Please tell me."

The old man paused, and sensing no dishonesty, accepted with a raise of one bushy brow. "As you wish. When this blade was crafted, which I would guess to be about eight and twelve hundred years ago, people were afraid of almost anything that went bump in the night. New religions were forming, making changes to the old ways, changing the way people thought and lived. These new faiths would have an effect on the way we thought about monsters and legends, as with all stories told to inspire fear or motivate into compliance. It was thought at one time there were demons of all shapes and sizes that walked by night in search of victims to corrupt or consume. Priests and clerics were constructing new weapons in an effort to combat these monsters that were thought to be of the greatest evil, wherever they could be found. I believe this knife is one such weapon. A weapon like this was passed from one owner to the next. It can never be taken from the owner ... or be used by any except its true owner."

"Why?"

"Because the weapon would always disappear from the one who had stolen it. Legend has it that all weapons of this kind have vanished from the world. If this knife is truly such a weapon, then you have a treasure that has no price to label its value. But more than this, this is a weapon that can never be lost. It will never be without you—or you without it—until you are ready to pass it along to the one you have chosen to succeed you."

"What kind of monsters do you think this knife would have been designed for?"

"Do you believe in demons that live with us in the cities? Or ghosts ... do you believe in them? Or maybe werewolves ... do you believe in the possibility of werewolves?"

"I don't believe in that stuff. Most of that is just Hollywood bunk," Bryan said, but he was unsure of the strength of his conviction.

"Maybe you should," the old man replied. He watched as Bryan placed the knife in his shirt.

"Thank you," Bryan said.

When the old man said nothing more, Bryan felt he had just been shown the door. As he stepped outside, an old voice in his mind said, "You're welcome."

Bryan turned and looked at the shop, but it wasn't a shop at all. It was an old landmark with a sign nailed across the front door, marking it for demolition. He felt an icy shiver run the length of his spine as he turned and marched quickly back to his apartment.

***

As the sun peeked through the trees, Dave Morrison lowered the brim of his cap to shield his eyes. He stepped carefully though the underbrush, watching for trap lines as he went, and he instructed his two trainees to follow his steps. His students, Christine Vainer and Cooper Hollander, had been sent from different locations as part of an apprentice program to participate in the studies and learn some of the investigative techniques in animal and big game management. Cooper was by far the more advanced student, hailing from some of the best schools on the West Coast. Christine showed real talent for getting her hands dirty, preferring to handle the discoveries she found along the way. She didn't have the advanced knowledge, but she was more intuitive about the job. Both students were attentive and curious, and they asked the right questions. Dave was happy to have both with him.

The morning had been uneventful, and the three had spent most of their time searching for scat and scratch markers along the trail that would indicate any game activity. The pickings had been slim, but there had been signs of recent traffic, perhaps by a trapper checking his lines. Dave started leading them off the main trails, more to the north than he would normally go, but he was hoping to find a sign he could use to introduce some of the problems he and his team had been having with the poaching in the area.

Dave pointed to the base of a tree a short distance ahead. "Okay, Cooper, what do you see there?"

Cooper knelt beside his teacher, lowered his cap to shade his eyes, and focused his attention. "I see scratch marks there at the base, but the ground is turned up as well, as if this was some sort of boundary marker." Cooper cringed as he caught the smell of something foul, but the sudden shift in behavior immediately caught Dave's undivided attention.

"Wait here," Dave whispered. He crept forward and caught the smell of rotting flesh, but there was something more. He moved forward to see how the ground had been disturbed. He was fearful of what might be lurking in the area, so he pulled his service revolver and cocked it. The ground wasn't just roughed up; it had been chewed up as if there had been one hell of a fight. He moved to a point where the ground dipped into a clearing, and then he stood up.

"Oh shit!" he said.

The scene was grim. There were the remnants of a campfire with two large poles rammed into the ground on either side. On one pole was an impaled human body; topping the other was a badly burned human skull that looked as if it had been smashed so that no teeth remained. There was no clothing on the body or around the camp, but a blackened badge glinted in the ashes of the fire. The body was not burned, but it was covered in deep lacerations as if some large animal had feasted on it. There was a great deal of bruising; most of the bones had been broken or crushed. The hands and feet had been removed, but they were nowhere around the camp as far as Dave could tell. He guessed the parts had been cast aside—and were probably long gone—but he would try to find what he could.

The ground around the camp had been disturbed; whoever had done this didn't care about the blood that would be spilled in committing this terrible act. Red stains could be seen as far as ten meters from the fire.

"Guys, bring the packs and put them at the base of the tree," Dave called. "Bring the rifles, gloves, and cameras down here."

The students trotted down the trail to the scene, and they were immediately shocked by what they saw. Christine proved to be the stronger person as Cooper moved to one side to vomit. He rinsed and wiped his mouth, and then he steadied himself to join the others.

"You okay?" Dave asked.

"Yeah, just never could handle the smell of burned flesh," Cooper responded. "What the hell is this?"

"This is a crime scene, and we are going to map, measure, shoot, and document everything we can," Dave said. "Playtime's over."

CHAPTER 10

▼

As usual, they decided to meet at Starbucks. Bryan bought a small coffee, but it tasted burnt. Jason and Allen soon arrived with cups of their own, but when it was time to leave, Bryan left his cup on the table almost untouched.

When the three friends stepped through the front reception area of their main place of employment, they were surprised to see very little activity going on. It didn't appear to be the usual hub of excitement that would be expected for the kind of business they were in. "What's going on?" Jason asked the receptionist.

"There seems to have been a change in office procedure," she responded between calls. "By the way, Mr. McReady is waiting for you in the main conference room."

"Mr. McReady?" Bryan whispered as he started toward the conference room. "This is starting to get my hackles up."

As they entered the room, Richard motioned Bryan to a chair. Bryan lowered himself in the chair as though he was about to sit on a scorpion. Jason and Allen took chairs on either side.

Richard folded his hands in front of him on the table; he sat for a long moment before speaking. "As I'm sure you know, we have finished our investigation. It seems there were facts about your business contacts you refused to share. I find this to be not acceptable to the policies and principles that have made this company successful."

"Richard, you had access to all our materials," Bryan started.

"Be silent and let me finish!" Richard barked. "The evidence we found connects you to sources not endorsed by this company. And there is evidence of misconduct and misappropriation of company resources. This brings to the table a whole new set of issues to be worked through, and it means we will initiate a new investigation regarding your work history."

"What the hell for?" Bryan was stunned by this implication of embezzlement. He looked at the somber faces of the rest of the attendees. Only Richard met his gaze. "What the hell are you doing, Richard?"

"Are you filing charges in this matter?" Allen asked.

"You are not being implicated here, Allen," Richard said.

"The hell I'm not! We were all part of the same projects … as a team. If you charge one, you charge us all."

"I think you need to keep a level head. You don't know what you're saying," Richard said.

"You need to think about what you're doing here," Allen said. "I will not stand by and let you tear Bryan apart for no reason. This is wrong, and you know it."

"Are the three of you of the same mind?" Richard asked.

The three friends looked at each other.

"Yes," Bryan said.

Richard said, "There comes a time when each man must face his darkest moment. It is this time when we are truly tested to the limits of our abilities."

"What the hell is all this blubbering bullshit? Get to the point," Bryan snapped.

"As you wish. This new investigation will be brought against the three of you, and whether or not you will be charged will be determined by the findings of this investigation. During the investigation, you will not be permitted access to company materials. You will not be permitted access to the property. Your licenses will be suspended indefinitely, and your computers will be confiscated until the conclusion of the investigation."

"What?" Bryan shouted.

"Furthermore, you are forbidden by law to conduct any trading, whether foreign or domestic, and your severance packages will be withheld until the conclusion of this investigation. After such time, I, as company president, will decide if it is appropriate to allow the imbursements to be issued to you for your time with the company."

"You bastard, you're just going to dump us in the street without even enough for a cup of coffee?" Jason asked.

"I did not ask you to support Bryan in this, but I'm glad we have a clear understanding. It has been determined that your services are no longer of use. And now your character must be called into question."

"You son of a bitch!" Bryan said. "You had all the time you needed to plan this. It's not enough to eliminate me from the company—you want to destroy me. You're going to steal my projects, my materials, everything I created and brought to this company." He could feel the fires of wrath swelling in him, and he stood so quickly that his chair bounced across the carpet behind him. Jason and Allen rose quickly and grabbed Bryan's arms to keep him from charging over the table at Richard. "You had no cause to do this—other than that I would have made you a lot of money—and now the money is all yours."

Richard ignored the remark and pushed a button on the phone at the center of the table. "Please inform security there will be three people needing an escort from the building."

"Right away, sir," a female voice responded.

The trio stared at their former boss. Bryan snatched a coffee cup and hurled it across the room. The cup exploded against the paneled wall behind Richard's head and showered the table with debris. The missile was meant to miss, but it had achieved the desired effect. Everyone in the room, except Richard, flinched at the crash and watched as the pieces skittered across the table. Bryan stared hard at Richard, and his expression turned to one of hatred.

"You will be paying for that coffee mug as well," Richard said, and his expression stated he had every intention of carrying out his threats. "Now, I believe you know the way out."

"Make no mistake, you fat barrel of monkey shit, I am coming back for you." Bryan turned and stormed out with his friends.

Allen waited until they were outside before grabbing Bryan's arm and forcing him to face his friend. "Are you sure that was a good idea?"

"Why should it matter now?" Bryan hissed.

"I guess it doesn't. What are you going to do now?" Allen asked

"I'm going to find out what's really going on here. The first thing to do is have a chat with that two-faced prick that started this whole mess."

"I know you're not going to see Brent alone," Jason said.

"And why not?"

"Because of the meeting we just had. If there is any conspiracy going on, Richard has already warned Brent. You'd be walking into a hornets' nest after somebody shakes it."

"I'll take my chances. I want answers and I intend to have a talk with him." Bryan was determined to do it alone—and make sure those responsible would fix this mess.

As Bryan walked down the sidewalk, he saw the familiar Malibu parked in front of the house. He stopped a short distance down the road to watch the house and the car in front of the main gate. There were two people in the car, but they didn't seem to be interested in much except the front door. They never left their comfortable chairs. Bryan walked to the alley as casually as he could. As expected, there was a car parked at the rear of the property in front of the garage; there was no way to access the backyard without being seen. The men in the car seemed content to stay where they were. He almost felt bad as he slithered into the next yard and silently hopped over the fence. Since breaking down the door was no longer an option, he played it cool, rapping lightly on the doorframe.

The door opened slowly. Brent's expression turned from one of surprise to discomfort when he saw Bryan's plastic smile.

"Well, won't you come in?" Brent asked sourly. He held the screen door open.

"Don't mind if I do. Thank you," Bryan said as he stepped through the door.

"Spare me your platitudes. You obviously didn't come here to be pleasant." Brent gently closed the door. "Would you like some coffee?"

"No, but thank you for the offer." Bryan dropped the smile. "I would like to find another job in shipping though, and I would appreciate any suggestions." He did nothing to hide the venom in his voice. It took all his strength to keep from lashing out at the human jackal in front of him.

"Don't you have to have a license to work as a shipping consultant?"

"Oh, that's right. All my licenses were suspended, but then you already know that. You set it up. Now I remember why I came here—to thank you for all you've done for me." Bryan's temper was getting warmer.

"Get to the point, then get out," Brent said.

Bryan stared at his antagonist for a long moment. "All right, I want my property back—all the discs, all the files—and I want to know why you did this."

"Why? Um, gee, I really think it's because I hate your guts. The way you paraded around the office after you landed that first big contract, and then the girls noticing you all over the place. I gotta tell ya, I really wanted some of that pussy action."

"Knock it off, asshole! I refuse to believe this was about you getting your carrot dipped. Just answer my question."

"You still don't get it, do you? I'm not giving you what you want. I don't have to tell you a goddamn thing. In fact, all I have to do is pick up the phone and my problems are solved." Brent moved to the phone at the counter.

"What the hell are you talking about?"

"I've got you by the balls now. You threatened my boss, and the fact that you got past those pathetic goons means I got you for breaking and entering. You go to jail now." Brent lifted the receiver, but he never got his hands on the buttons.

"Bastard!" Bryan screamed as he jumped. Brent dropped the receiver and reached for a kettle on the stove. Bryan was moving too fast to avoid the attack, and he took the kettle across the left side of his face. He howled in pain as he fell back and slammed his head into a cupboard door as he hit the floor.

Brent reached for a baseball bat in the closet. "Think you can come here and make demands in my house?" He swung hard, and the bat made a dull thud as it hit Bryan's rib cage. Again Bryan howled.

Bryan felt the back of his head and winced, and then he turned and looked at the fresh blood on the cupboard door. He felt his side, and though it hurt, no bones were broken. He could feel himself changing, could hear the blood rushing through his veins, but he no longer cared.

Brent swung again, but this time Bryan was able to dodge, and the bat bounced harmlessly off the cupboard door.

Bryan regained his feet as Brent raised the bat for another attack. This time, Bryan caught the bat and ripped it from Brent's grip. The bat flew across the room and rattled on the hardwood floor. Brent punched hard and connected with Bryan's jaw, but Bryan wasn't affected by the attack. He could feel the rage inside, could feel his muscles straining against his shirt. His blood pulsed like thunder in his ears. He grabbed Brent by his lapels and, pulling and turning at the same time, sent Brent crashing into the closet door. The door splintered into a cloud of toothpicks. Bryan knew this fight would have to end quickly. The watchers outside would soon be alerted to the ruckus.

Brent pulled himself from the wreckage of his closet. Finding a barbecue fork, he jumped and thrust it toward Bryan's throat. Bryan easily caught the outstretched arm and squeezed, feeling the bones snap in his iron grip. Brent squealed one last time as Bryan sank his claws deep into Brent's flesh. He raised Brent off the floor, and with one final thrust, he sank his claws into the chest cavity, gripping the heart and ripping it free. Bryan could smell the sweet odor of blood. He was exhilarated as he dropped the body—and the heart—and leapt out the back door.

As expected, the slamming car doors could be heard as more potential victims were milling about to investigate. Bryan retreated to the shadows and waited for the guards to pass, and then he jumped over the fence. He was able to avoid being seen by staying in the shadows and using the back alleys until he was close to home. He noticed a police cruiser parked close to the front door of his building. Two uniforms were talking to Bryan's quiet neighbor. Home was no place to be now; he would go see Jason.

The excitement and euphoric power stayed with him as he ran. He felt free as never before—even as he thought about what he had done. He felt the city around him, could smell everything around him, and it made him feel like an emperor. He knew his time in the city was coming to an end.

Bryan banged loudly at Jason's back door. As soon as the door opened, Bryan wasted no time. "Jason, I need your help." He was still wearing his torn clothing, and he had done nothing to hide the fresh blood on his hands.

"I just got the phone call, and I—"

"Jason!" Bryan shouted as he stepped through the door. "He's dead."

"You know?"

"Know? Know what?" Bryan stammered and stumbled back. "I mean, it shouldn't even be news yet."

"Bryan, what are you talking about? I just got the call from Lyle."

"Lyle? What did he want?"

"John McCauley is dead. A hiker found his body about five miles north of the village. The cabin was hit too. Somebody trashed it good."

"Damn. I hope he wasn't killed because of something I did." Bryan took a deep breath and wandered into the kitchen to sit down. "This is all happening too fast."

"Wait a minute. You said he's dead. Who's dead? Bryan, what did you do?"

"I killed Brent." Bryan tried to settle the excitement of the past hour. "This is all going to connect, and Richard will stop at nothing to bury me."

"Jesus Christ, Bryan. Do you have any idea what you've done? How is anyone going to know we all weren't there? You have to talk to somebody."

"They will know you weren't there."

"How can you be sure?"

"Because I ripped his heart out with my bare hands. Everything there shows the work of one, not more. How many people do you know that have the ability to do that?" Bryan held up his hands to show the blood of his victim.

"Holy shit!" Jason whispered as he took a step back. "Okay, this is real."

"Get it now? I did something, and I don't know how. I changed, and it felt great, and it wasn't me. I'm in real trouble here, and the cops are the least of my concerns."

"Um, yeah, you gotta get out of here."

"I know that, Jason!"

"So what are we going to do?"

"There's only one thing for me to do. If I stay, this is going to become a media circus. I will not give Richard any more reason to hurt you and Allen. Besides, Allen doesn't know yet, and I'd like to keep it that way."

"You know he wouldn't approve of that."

"I know. That's why I have to go alone."

"Alone? Go where alone?"

"I have to go back to Pink Mountain."

"What the hell for? I thought you had all the answers you needed from this trip."

"I was wrong. There's something up there. There seems to be something more I need to find out. Whatever it is, it was important enough to get John killed. I will not do that to you or Allen. Besides, at worst, the police will be looking for me—not you and Allen."

"You have to tell Allen."

"No, he doesn't need to know."

"Do you want him to find out on the news after the manhunt has been announced? He deserves better than that. If you don't tell him, I will."

"No, Jason, let it go."

Bryan got up to leave, but Jason grabbed him by the arm and spun him around.

"You stubborn asshole! You don't get to just walk away like this. And you don't get to leave us behind. We swore an oath together. All of us are in this whether you like it or not. You want to go back on the mountain, fine, but you are not going alone."

"You are not going to let this go, are you?"

"No," Jason grunted.

"If we go, there's a chance you won't like what we find. I need to know what the hell is wrong with me. And it might be something that kills us all. I killed a man, and I can face that."

Jason refused to let go.

"You can't be involved in this."

Bryan tried to pull away, but Jason held his grip.

"Okay, so what do we do now?" Bryan said.

"We do what we have to. Have you unpacked yet?"

"Yes, but I can't go home. The police are already there."

"Go get cleaned up and help me pack. We'll go to Allen's and get some stuff. Leave your wallet and everything that can be traced. I'll get a change of clothes for you."

"The police will have put out reports at all transit centers and flight centers by now. How are we going to get out of the city without being seen?"

"Leave that to me."

Jason spoke briefly on the phone while Bryan cleaned up and puttered around, waiting for the next move. Jason hung up, gathered as much cash as he had, and picked up the phone again. "Allen, have you unpacked?"

"No," Allen said.

"Good, get your stuff together and meet me at False Creek Marina in one hour. We're going back on vacation for a while."

Jason unplugged everything and put a pack together for Bryan. "Allen is going to make sure everything is secure before we leave. He'll meet us at the marina."

Bryan nodded. "Oh shit!"

"What?"

"We have to go back to my place. I have to get my knife."

"I thought it was just a collectible. Why is it so important?"

"I don't know," Bryan lied. "I just know I have to get it before we leave."

Jason stared at Bryan for a moment. "Okay. I'll get the knife—and then we go to Allen."

As expected, a car was in front of the building, and a man in uniform stood near the entrance. Jason parked his Honda at the end of the block so they could watch from a safe distance. The officer got into the car with his partner. Since there didn't seem to be a sense of urgency, Bryan figured they would stake out the place until the officers were called away.

"Where do you keep the knife?" Jason asked.

"I always keep it hidden. There is a false panel in my closet behind the rack at about chest level. Use the side door to get in. And be nice to Jim. He sleeps behind the bins there."

Bryan handed over his keys. A few minutes later, Jason returned to the car.

"What took you so long?"

"I talked with Jim. I gave him ten bucks to argue with the cops about somebody stealing his shopping carts. It gave me the time I needed to slip out the parking exit."

"Clever. I never thought of that."

They pulled away and left the streetlights to burn away the increasing shadow.

"Once we get back there, you take the lead," Jason said.

"How do we get there?"

"Don't worry. It's all arranged. A friend is going to borrow my car for a while. We'll go up the coast for a bit, and then I'll take his car the rest of the way. We'll be there in two days."

"Okay, the first thing for me to do is find Lyle and find out what happened. I don't know what else to do until I do that."

It was almost dark by the time they reached the marina. Allen was waiting for them at the front gate. Allen and Bryan pulled the packs from the car as Jason boarded the boat to check all the necessities. The boat was just a day cruiser, but it was large enough to hold six people. It was inconspicuous enough to avoid raising any suspicions. When Bryan looked at the dock, he saw a hooded figure in the shadows. He watched as Jason nodded, and the figure nodded in response.

Allen stowed the gear and made sure all the ropes were undone. "Bryan, can you get the stern locks?"

Bryan did as instructed, and soon they were floating in the channel. From there, it was just a matter of getting far enough away from the dock before the engines could be engaged. When Bryan looked back at the dock, Jason's car was gone.

CHAPTER 11

▼

Caution tape was being put all around the backyard, and the area around the back door was being kept clear in anticipation of the forensics crew. Detective Richard Lee was nursing a smoke at the back gate and waiting for the team to arrive. Other officers ran around the scene, taking notes and formulating stories of their own. He brushed ashes from the sleeve of his blue blazer as the team arrived and removed tool kits from their vehicles.

"I thought you guys would never get here," he said. "Couldn't you have at least brought me some coffee?"

The first to enter the scene was a short, stocky man named Edgar Collack. He stopped at the door and casually looked inside at the wreckage. "Seems like there is always something new I haven't seen. I thought I had seen it all." His olive skin and accent suggested a European background. Edgar was the team leader.

The other four from his team busied themselves with taking photos and notes. The pathologist waited outside until he was called in.

Rick offered a smoke to Edgar and the pathologist. When they refused, he pocketed the smokes. "Nothing has been touched yet. The rest of the house has been checked and cleared. It's all yours whenever you're ready."

Edgar nodded and focused his attention on the door frame. "It doesn't look like there was a forced entry here. Jamie, will you take some photos of the patio before you go in?"

A tall brunette shot several angles of the patio and door, and then gave way for the pathologist to start.

Mathew Kepperri was a product of rich upbringing and appeared too young for the job. "Okay, let's have a look," he said. He stepped through the door to examine the position of the body. "Oh, this is messy. Well, I think we can be sure of the cause of death. Whoever wanted this person dead didn't just want to kill—there was a point to be made here." Mathew moved easily around the scene, and his thin frame displayed a surprising strength.

"How do you know?" Rick asked.

"Because of the way the body is shown here. The body is not displayed, and there is no tampering that would show anything but rage. It takes strength to rip a man's heart out. And look at this forearm here." Mathew lifted the crushed arm, still holding the barbecue fork. "You see the way it was crushed, the way the bones were snapped? It takes an amazing amount of strength to do something like this. I think your killer is a large man. The indentations on the arm—or claw marks if you will— suggest anger, and your dead man here is not small. Look at the way the door has been smashed in. This man was not pushed. He was thrown. You are looking for a killer who is large and very pissed off." Mathew dug out a notepad and started taking notes. "I'll know more when I get him back to the lab. In the meantime, if you plan to go after the person who did this, I would advise extreme caution. This person has no compunctions about killing. And he will kill again."

"You seem to have a talent for recognizing the worst in a situation," Rick said.

"Well, this job wasn't what my father wanted, but when I realized forensics is where I wanted to be, he cut off my schooling. All sarcasm aside, I enjoy the work."

"Thank you."

Rick stepped outside to let the team finish working. He hated ugly cases because they usually meant turning up something he wished he'd left alone. "Edgar, I don't think we're going to get any calls that will demand your attention elsewhere. Will you let me know when this is done?"

"Sure thing, boss. What are you going to do?"

"I'm going to make a few calls to see if this guy had any connections—or enemies—that would want him this dead. I'll be back in a few hours. I don't think our killer is done yet, but I hope I'm wrong."

"So do I," Edgar said. They both knew the nightmare had just begun.

The station was a hub of activity. Extra officers had been called in for a series of accidents downtown, and several bar brawls had to be broken up. Rick was on his way past the front desk when the officer hailed him.

"We got something here." The officer held up a portable chip with a note attached.

"What is this?"

"Edgar dropped this off, and I got word back on a couple things. The interviews pointed to someplace called Pink Mountain, and there was some kind of disturbance at the apartment you sent those cars to."

"What kind of disturbance?"

"Some old guy was complaining about stuff … something about a stolen shopping cart."

Rick thought for a moment. "He's already gone," he said.

"Sir?"

"Bryan Delman is already gone, and I think I know where. Thank you. Keep an eye on those addresses."

"Also, there was someone named McReady here."

"Yeah. He said something about a project his company was working on—maybe on this thing."

"This is all beginning to make sense. I'll get Strassman to rip this apart," Rick said. He found Lina Strassman easily enough; if she wasn't in the computer lab, she was close to a vending machine. Her blue hair was always swaying to some form of music. Today it was Roxette. She always seemed out of place, but in front of a computer screen, she was a regular Stephen Hawking.

Rick waited for her to turn around, and she quickly turned her headphones down when she saw she had company. "Uh, sorry, boss."

"Don't worry about it," he said. "I need to find out what this is."

"Where did it come from?"

"A crime scene on the other side of town."

"No probs. Is this priority?"

"Yes, please."

"Okay, give me a few hours. I'll crack it." She put the chip in her purse along with her portable radio.

"I will call you later to find out what's on it."

When Rick called her four hours later, she had her music down low enough to hear everything around her. "What did you figure out?"

"Well, the chip wasn't that hard to figure out," Lina said. "There were no codes or encryptions to bypass. It seems this thing has everything you would need to know about shipping companies: times, market rates, and exchange rates. All the codes that are listed are done in a straightforward format, so it's easy to understand. Typically this is the kind of information you would use to work overseas without actually being there, especially if you were some kind of power broker who would be dealing in high-end computer equipment or telecommunications. There's even a list of close to a thousand different shipping ports and customs offices in several countries for more effective trading based on what the world markets are doing at the time of the transactions."

"What exactly does that mean?"

"It means you could plug this into any decent computer and be capable of moving cargo and information at an accelerated rate and still have access to any trading port in Asia. You could trade anything on the world markets at the exact time of the market fluctuations and have the versatility to adjust to the changes as they happened. Whoever created this program put a lot of thought into it. This kind of information would take a long time to gather. If I used this for myself, I could make myself a millionaire in six months without the intervention of any company to stop me from what I was doing."

"Jesus, no wonder he wanted this so bad. If you could use this to make millions without a company to back you, someone with access to a larger software trading company could make billions and corner the markets. How do you know this stuff?"

"Business classes—and a broker friend of mine."

"Well done."

This answered some questions, but it still left much to figure out. Whoever had killed Brent didn't care about leaving the program behind. This was not about getting back what was stolen; it was about taking care of a loose end. He knew he had to go to Pink Mountain to find out why Bryan was there.

CHAPTER 12

▼

Bryan had a lot to think about on the way up, and he wasn't sure if it was this or the long hours that made him feel the pressure of a headache starting. He turned on no lights—and there was no moonlight. He felt more comfortable, but he wasn't sure why. He was still trying to relax around midnight when he heard a light rapping by his motel door. He opened the door and looked out to the walkway, and then the sidewalk.

"Bryan," Lyle whispered.

Bryan saw Lyle in the shadows. "How long have you been standing there?"

"It doesn't matter," Lyle replied. "Get your stuff. You're not staying here tonight."

"But—"

"The bill has been paid, and your friends are waiting for us in the truck. We don't have much time." Lyle stepped from the shadows and disappeared.

Bryan grabbed his pack and locked the door behind him. He threw his pack in the back and climbed into the cab. "I don't—"

"Quiet!" Lyle snapped. They drove for another ten minutes before Lyle spoke again. "My apologies, but I needed to be sure no one could hear. You will be staying at my cabin tonight. I'll explain everything when we get there."

"What can you tell me about John?" Bryan asked.

"Not much."

"Do you know who did it?"

"No," Lyle said.

"You're lying."

Lyle looked at his passenger. "You're right, but then you also know why. This is the kind of situation that can be used to fuel a coup against the council. I have had to work quickly to keep this silent so exactly that situation would be prevented. No one in the village knows what happened. It has to stay that way for now."

"I don't understand," Bryan said. "What does John have to do with the council?"

"Nothing, but the investigation that would follow would bring authorities here. That would cause enough fear for those who are already running. Before the council can be told what's going on, they have to be protected from engagements on two different front lines. And engagement with the law at this point is far more dangerous. John's death will be answered for, but not until I can be sure someone won't overthrow the authority of the council to solidify his powerbase."

"Someone? You mean Dario."

Lyle's look confirmed Bryan's suspicion.

"This is happening too fast." Bryan was beginning to understand what was going on at the village, but he still had to figure out his own problems before he could help Lyle. He tried to focus his mind on staying awake, but the headache and the long hours were catching up to him. Soon he slipped into an uneasy slumber. He had no idea how long he slept, and when Jason shook him, he saw nothing recognizable. "Where are we?" he mumbled.

"We're almost there," Lyle said. He pulled the truck onto a dirt track, pitted and rough with disrepair. After ten minutes, he stopped the truck in front of a dark cabin. "You guys need rest. We'll talk more in the morning."

The cabin appeared larger than the one Jason had taken him to, but he didn't care as long as there was a soft spot for his aching head. He helped Jason carry the bags inside and saw the sleeping arrangements had already been set for the visitors. Within minutes, he was out cold on his bed.

The smell of pine and cedar filled the air. Bryan saw gray shadows swirling in the soft wind. The fog was heavy, and visibility was impaired after only a few feet. The air was chilled; it was as though the stones in the area had absorbed all the warmth. Bryan's hearing was the only sense that offered any identification of direction. He moved slowly through the fog, unsure of what direction to follow. He tried to focus his vision on something solid, but nothing came into view. *If this is a forest, why can't I see any trees or other vegetation?*

Bryan heard footsteps around him, but he could not determine the source. He saw nothing through the white wall that blinded him. He took a deep breath and tried to calm his mind, concentrating on his hearing. The footsteps were coming from everywhere and nowhere. He sniffed the air and detected the smell of something not human. He didn't recognize the smell, but his defensive instinct increased as his fear increased. His claws were as sharp as talons, and his teeth were sharper.

Shapes and shadows moved quickly through the mist; the fog had thinned imperceptibly. The shapes moved as though they were combatants almost within striking distance. He pictured each shape in his mind as he watched the shapes moving. He sniffed the air again; the smells cleared his vision. When the mist shifted subtly in front of his searching eyes, he saw thin, shadowy stands of trees. He tried to move closer to the tree line, but the faster he moved, the more distant the trees seemed to be. The shadows started to move closer.

As Bryan ran, he heard growls, snaps, and snarls. There was electricity in the air. As he reached out with his mind, the air showed him what his eyes couldn't. He saw trees and ground clutter. As he watched the shadowy images, he thought he saw them changing—or was he changing himself?

They appeared to be wolves and men. Bryan felt their hunger and rage. He tasted metal as his own rage and hatred increased. He tightened his muscles in preparation for an attack. As the shadows moved closer, every face he looked at was his own. As the first attack was launched, he shifted, lost his balance, and hit the ground hard. He stopped thinking about the terrain as he readied himself for the next strike. He collided hard with the next opponents, and he raked his claws at their throats as they reached for his. He felt a hard strike on the back of his head, and a blinding flash forced his eyes closed. When he opened his eyes, Jason and Lyle were working to keep him pinned to the floor.

Bryan stopped resisting. "What the hell is going on?"

"You tell me!" Lyle snarled. "All I know is I hear you snarling and snapping. When I come in here, I see that my room is a mess."

He let go of Bryan's arm and raised himself painfully to a standing position so Bryan could do the same. Jason held onto Bryan as he got up, and he stared at Bryan's arms.

"What the hell just happened to me?" Bryan asked.

"I'd say by the look of this room, you were having a night terror," Lyle said. "You are going to rebuild my room, by the way."

The vanity mirror was smashed, and broken glass was all over the room. The pillows were ripped beyond repair, and the bedspread was torn to pieces. A broken clock on the floor showed the time as just after six. The bed had been moved, perhaps as a result of Bryan trying to resist the enemies. There was blood on the walls, and his hands had been beaten raw.

"Holy shit! What is happening to me?"

"I think you know … and I think you have a good idea of the kind of trouble you're in. It's what brought you back here," Lyle said. "There's one question you haven't asked."

"What do I do now?"

Lyle stared at Bryan. "I'd say it's time for you to take a hike."

"What?" Bryan asked.

"Don't worry. I'm not sending you home. I have a friend coming. He'll take you."

"Take me where?"

"To see someone who can help you. The old man is the only one who can help you now."

"Wait a minute," Jason said. "What about Allen and me? We came here to help Bryan through this … together."

"You can't help him now," Lyle said. "Besides, you two and I have our own tasks to manage. While Bryan is gone, someone has to deal with the details of John's death. I need your help for that."

There was a knock on the door, and Lyle shuffled through the debris to admit his visitor.

"Is that clock accurate?" Bryan asked.

"No, you saw to that," Jason said. "It's nearly seven."

"Take it easy. I didn't do this on purpose."

"I know. I'm sorry," Jason said.

"Where's Allen?"

"He's making breakfast He decided to play it safe and let us handle you. I'd say your little problem just became world class."

"Don't worry about him," a voice said as they entered the kitchen.

Jason and Bryan turned to see a new face join the party.

"I know you. You were at the village," Bryan said.

"Yes, my name is Henry." He still wore the green overcoat and heavy boots. Though he was young, his face showed signs of wear.

"Where are we going?" Bryan asked.

"I will take you to see the old man," Henry said.

"Henry is the only one who can take you. He can take you on routes even I don't know," Lyle said. "If someone tries to follow, Henry can make sure no one will find you."

"How long will it take us to get there?"

"Two days," Henry said.

"What do I need to take with me?"

"You have all you need, but don't forget your dagger," Henry said.

"How did you know about that?"

"You will find there is little that can be hidden from me. Get ready. We leave in one hour." Henry walked out to get his pack in order.

When breakfast was ready, Bryan ate little so he would have the extra time he needed to square things away. He found he had little appetite anyway. He secured his pack, and his guide urged him to say his good-byes quickly. "I don't know how long I'll be gone," Bryan said.

"You'll be gone as long as it takes to get this sorted out," Allen said. "We'll be waiting in the village when you get back."

Bryan turned to Jason. "Look, man—"

"Don't," Jason said. "We took an oath. Go do what you have to do."

The three friends clasped hands for less than a minute, but it was the strongest bond Bryan had ever felt. He let go when he was gently nudged by his guide. Bryan turned and walked into the wild.

***

Lyle parked the truck a hundred meters from the entrance to the village. Lyle, Jason, and Allen piled out of the truck and began their search for the leader of the village. The few people still there busied themselves with chores or overdue repairs. A few people were working the fields behind the main hall. It gave the impression that most of the partygoers had gone home—or to other parts of the world—and left the place with only enough crew to keep up appearances. Lyle saw no one taking note of the visitors until they were interrupted from their work.

Lyle tapped a young man's shoulder. He was busy painting one of the outbuildings. "Excuse me, can you tell me where I might find Dario? It is a matter of some urgency."

"Try behind the chapel. I think he was fixing something there." The young man responded without turning.

Lyle found Dario working on a sign for the next season. "We need to talk," he said.

Dario looked up with surprise. "To what do I owe the honor of this visit?" The question was pleasant enough, but Lyle could tell there was acid in Dario's voice.

"By now you have heard about the ranger."

"I heard there was an incident that unfortunately resulted in the man's death. I am sorry to hear of it. I did like the man," Dario said.

"That's what we need to talk about."

"Why? I heard it was an accident."

"That's because I made sure the media didn't know the whole story … and because I know what really happened to John."

Dario's expression immediately soured, and he dropped his tools. "You had best be sure of your statements. Have you any proof?"

"That is what you will find out tonight. Call the meeting—and then we'll talk."

Dario scanned their faces for any sign of weakness, but their faces were blank. "Why should I do this?"

"Because if you don't, I will have the authorities up here after I set this place on fire," Lyle said flatly.

"Then we will talk with the council tonight," Dario said. He was left to return to his work.

The night was warm, but there would be no festivities or welcoming fire. The attendees would discuss what would happen the next season and relay the news that was important to the village's future. Lanterns in the main hall lent a surreal ambience to the place. Shadows danced and moved across the walls as the lanterns were put on their pedestals. A single brazier glowed at one end of the room, giving off a pleasant aroma of pine and cinnamon. There were ten people on the council and about forty in the audience. Comments were whispered about why the council had been called a week earlier than usual. There were rumors and speculation about what might happen. Most of the time, people were happy to let the council do its work uninterrupted so they didn't have to attend these meetings. This time, everybody wanted to know what was going on.

Lyle knew one man would not let the opportunity to argue any point pass him by. Dario was the last to enter, and he took his place at the head of the council. As soon as everyone was seated, the minutes of the last meeting were read. The introduction to the next season had to be given before other business was invited to the floor.

Lyle waited to be addressed by the council. When Allen and Jason stood to join him, he gently urged them to remain in their seats.

"There has been activity outside the village the council should know about," Lyle started. "A man has been killed by one who is not part of the council but who is subject to the direction of it."

"This is a serious accusation," Dario said. "I hope you have evidence to back this claim. If you do, the council will see what evidence there is and decide what to do from there."

"No. I will decide what to do if the council chooses not to act," Lyle countered.

"This is improper!" Dario was visibly irritated, but the others on the council looked on with suspicion and curiosity. "You have no power to influence the council in its actions. What gives you the right to address the council in such a manner?"

"I have the right to see justice done for the victim. John McCauley was ripped apart, and his parts were hung from the trees like a curtain for the entire world to see. There is only one who kills like this. Anton Bender will answer for this crime."

"And I will kill you next!" Anton stomped forward from the back of the room, causing all in the room to turn to the source of the angry voice.

Lyle turned to face his challenger. He was not ready to kill another inside the hall, but if he was attacked, he would defend himself with lethal intent.

"Stand down!" Dario shouted. His words vibrated off the walls, and all inside the hall were amazed by the power of the old man's voice. Both combatants turned to face Dario. "There will be no blood spilled in this hall," he growled.

"The accused is here. Will he answer?" Lyle asked.

Dario turned his attention to Anton. "Is what this man says true?"

"Yes," Anton answered without hesitation. His gaze never left his opponent, and he did nothing to hide his hatred for Lyle.

"Why did you kill the ranger?" Dario asked.

"Because he was going to see the old man. He was going to expose us."

"Fool! You have exposed us! The ranger would have exposed you and your business. I wanted the ranger unharmed—not dead. You were supposed to kill another."

This prompted looks from the rest of the council, and Lyle turned to Dario with a look of disgust. "You knew. All I did was keep the story from being heard. Bryan was the one he was supposed to kill."

"Yes, he was the one," Dario said. "He could have carried our secret to areas we could not reach."

Lyle stared at Dario. "Bryan is the threat you fear. I should have known. You are too late. This place is no longer a secret. Rumors will spread like a disease, and there will be more people sniffing around. I will contain the story no longer, and you will have to answer for that as well. Now Bryan is beyond your reach."

"You know nothing." Dario said. "I still call the rules here. The village survives because I say it does. Why should I believe you?"

"Because Bryan has already killed his first. If you check the news, you will see there is a manhunt for him. Even if you were to kill Bryan now, it would change nothing. If you were wiser, you might have realized your mistake before it got to this point. Besides, this council is ruled by vote, not by law. The council decides what is right for the village, not you. Perhaps it has come time for another to lead the council."

"Are you challenging for leadership?"

"No, but I will wait for the council's decision. This matter must still be resolved."

All the council members but Dario sat mute. No one volunteered to add to the discussion.

Dario said, "Tell me where Bryan is so I can help clean up this mess."

Lyle said, "You do not command the council to act. If the council can't rule in the proper manner, then I say the council is impotent, and the village will not survive another season." Lyle turned and walked toward the door with Allen and Jason in tow. He stopped before the door to address the council one last time. "This is your mess to clean up. I will have nothing more to do with it."

The doors closed with a loud boom that echoed through the hall.

On the way back to his lodge, Lyle said, "Dario will want to pull all his wild cards now to keep from falling apart before the authorities arrive to investigate John's death."

"It seems all you did was to put Bryan on the spot. Anton knows Bryan was here, and he knows roughly where we are. Doesn't that put us in danger?" Jason asked.

"There are things about this situation you can't understand. By now, Bryan is well on his way with the best damn tracker this side of the Rockies. And as far as you two being vulnerable, you are safer with me than with anyone else on the mountain. Dario's position is in jeopardy. I attacked Dario's leadership in front of the council. Now he will have to prove his abilities if he is to continue to lead the village. The only way for him to do that is to see that the right decisions are made—and to stand down any challenges that come before him. In fact, the only wild card I'm concerned about is Anton. He's the one I haven't figured out yet."

"Anton scares me," Allen said. "Based on our previous encounter, I can see him coming after us at earliest opportunity—even if he was not given orders to. You even said he's a rogue."

"That's the one thing I'm counting on," Lyle said.

"What? Why?" Jason asked.

"Anton knows you two are with me—and he knows Bryan is on his way to see the old man—but he doesn't know how long Bryan has been out there or which route Henry will take. Anton knows he can't catch Bryan now. He failed to stop Bryan, and that was Dario's motivation from the beginning. Dario fears Bryan most of all. Bryan is the one who must challenge Dario for leadership, whether he wants to or not. We have known this up here for a long time. What we did tonight is buy Bryan some time."

"Anton has killed before. What makes you think he won't do it again? Why would he stop now?" Allen asked.

"Anton killed John because Dario sent him to stop John. Well, John was stopped. The council was able to ignore it because the others he killed didn't have anything to do with the village. If an investigation ever came to the village, the council would bury it. If Anton tries anything tonight, the council should, by right, hand Anton over to the authorities. And Anton knows that too. Anton will not come after us unless he is ordered to. Dario is the only one who can defy the council at this point. Anton doesn't have the strength to challenge Dario."

"What makes Bryan so important?" Allen asked.

"Have you noticed that Bryan is smaller than you, but he's much more powerful?"

"He's always been like that, so what?"

"I was hoping Bryan would be here before we had this conversation." Lyle took a deep breath. "We've been waiting for Bryan to come back. He's not the same as you and Jason. I hope I'm wrong, but I think you will learn the truth tonight."

"So what do we do now?" Allen asked.

"We wait. Bryan will take care of the rest."

There was so much that Lyle could not say to his new friends because his credibility would be tested. Trust was most important. Lyle, and few others, knew the prophecy written so long ago. The time of that prophecy was now—and Bryan was the central element—but it was not time to reveal its truth to his guests.

CHAPTER 13

▼

Bryan and his guide hiked the trail in silence. Neither man felt the need for conversation. He'd had a great deal to think about since his flight from the city, and the silence helped to keep his mind focused. Henry, though helpful enough to point out the hazards along the trail, remained taciturn. Bryan decided not to push the matter, preferring to wait until his guide was open to the possibility of conversation.

When it came time to set camp for the night, Henry's orders were crisp, and his manner was terse. There would be no fire—no sign that could be used to track them or identify their destination. They pitched their tents in silence, and Bryan thought it the right time to take a risk.

"Can I ask you a question?"

"No," Henry said without looking up.

"You don't talk much, do you?"

Henry glared in silence. It seemed that it was all the conversation Bryan would get. Bryan sighed and settled in for the night. They would be up again in six hours.

Bryan was awakened by the sound of his tent rustling as the zipper was being pulled down. The door flaps were opened, and Bryan saw Henry's shadow.

"What time is it?"

"Four. Time to get ready." Henry raised himself and walked to his pack. He already had his equipment loaded, and he was removing any signs of their presence.

Bryan got his things together and was dressed in a matter of minutes. As he finished the last of his preparations, Henry tossed him a pemmican bar. He caught the offered breakfast and smiled his thanks.

Since the ground was still warm, thick fog gathered around their knees. The light of a new day was making its slow crawl over the hills, and a light breeze was moving across the land. There was soon enough light to see that the trail was about to get rough. Henry sat patiently on a rock as Bryan finished his preparations and his breakfast. There was little about Henry for Bryan to admire, but his stoic strength told him his guide was a man without illusion.

Bryan found the situation a bit troubling, but short of asking where they were, he could find no words to open a conversation. He finished his meal and mounted his pack as he took his place behind his guide.

After a few hours of hard travel, Bryan's shoulders began to burn from carrying his pack, and he tried to focus on the sounds around him to keep his mind from the pain. When they reached the first stop, Henry gathered some moss to place on Bryan's bare shoulders. It did little more than soothe the burn a bit, but Bryan was thankful for the gesture.

When they reached their second stop, the day had become hot enough to drain the strength from the most experienced hiker. They sipped water slowly so there would be no cramping muscles to deal with later.

"How much farther do we travel today?" Bryan asked.

"I go with you to the next stop ... then you must go alone."

"Are you sure?"

"I have traveled this route many times. It is the way it must be. The old man will know you are here, and he will meet you soon enough."

Henry signaled that it was time to push on. When the trail became rockier, he centered his attention on his footsteps. There was no room to examine his emotions or any reasons for self-incrimination.

After three hours, they stopped at a rocky outcropping that offered a view of the last leg of the journey. They were much higher than Bryan would have suspected. There were rock walls and jutting sections on either side of the trail. The trail dropped sharply, but increased in height and degree of incline further up. After that, Bryan could see no farther.

"Look there." Henry pointed to a snag of trees a thousand meters away. The trees were difficult to see clearly in the sunlight, but Bryan thought they were curled in the shape of a hand.

"Is that a finger?" Bryan asked.

"Follow it."

Farther up, Bryan saw an odd rock formation. It was part of an overhang, but it looked as though the formation was not supposed to be there. Perhaps his eyes were seeing a trick of the light, but it looked like a welcome mat. "What is that?"

"That is where you must go. I can go no further."

"How far is it to that formation?"

"About four hours. Make your way to the finger. Your senses will take you the rest of the way. At the rock formation, wait for the old man. He will take you where you need to go."

"What are you going to do?"

"I will go back to the hotel. I will be back here when you are ready to leave." Henry picked up his gear and started back down the trail without a word of farewell.

After his guide was out of sight, Bryan picked up his gear and continued as he had been directed. The hike was much more difficult than he had anticipated. Before long, he was sweating and nearing the point of exhaustion, but he managed to make it to the snag of trees in one piece. The snag appeared to be in front of a rock wall where the trail abruptly ended. When he examined the snag, the cracked and bleached wood appeared to be formed, blown over, or pressed down by many years of cold and wind. The wood blended subtly into the environment. Though it might have seemed magical, it was a completely natural phenomenon.

Having solved that riddle, it was time to move on. He sipped his water and thought about Henry's words about letting his senses guide him. He concentrated on his hearing, but nothing happened or gave him direction. He sat down and focused his mind on nothing, trying to allow his mind to be carried away by the sounds of the forest. In his mind, he saw himself climbing a tree. A few meters to the north, there was another trail.

When he opened his eyes, he knew where he had to go, but he couldn't see where the trail might begin. There was only rock in front of him, but it was too difficult to climb. When he stopped to listen, it seemed that the trees were talking to him. When he heard the word "door" in his mind, he knew what to do. When he reached forward, the rock in front of him was another illusion. He moved around the giant boulders to find the trail. He continued on, wondering at the marvelous complexity of nature—and how easily he had been deceived by it.

The trail became more indefinite, tangled with roots, making the hike more difficult. Bryan found his way only because he remembered which direction to travel. By the time he got to his next stop, there was no longer a trail. The closer he got, the more the trees closed in.

When he reached the overhang, he settled in to wait for his host. Until he pulled off his pack, he had no idea how exhausted he was. His shoulders burned and ached, and his leg muscles quivered and throbbed. He decided to find a comfortable spot to rest for a moment. Soon the world began to slip away, and his senses gave in to sleep. From a distance, another pair of eyes watched with great interest.

Bryan woke to the sounds of a campfire, and he felt the warmth and comfort as if he was in a room at the Hilton. When he opened his eyes, he was in a large open field. The trees had been cleared in the area, but he didn't recognize any landmarks.

"Nice to see you awake," a voice said. The voice was deep, powerful, and dry from many years of seasonal exposure.

Bryan looked around for the source, but he saw nothing. "Who are you?"

"I am the one you have traveled so far to find."

"Why have I been drawn to this place?" He regretted the question as soon as he asked it.

"If that is the question you need to ask, I suggest you turn back now. You should be able to make it back to town in three days. You know the way."

"I … forgive me." Bryan searched his mind for the next question—the question that could not be answered. The time had come to cast away the shell of his reality that dictated what his mind would accept as real in order to accept what would have been thought impossible. "How long have you been waiting for me?"

A frail man with a white staff stepped out of the shadows. Bryan was startled by the old man's sudden appearance—and upset that he hadn't seen him earlier.

"I have waited many seasons," the old man said. The wrinkled face betrayed no weakness, and the compassion in his voice carried the wisdom of ages past. "Don't be troubled by your inability to see. That is a trick I will show you in time."

"Then it is time," Bryan said as he felt the scar on his arm.

"Yes. You have come home." The old man sat beside Bryan at the fire. "All will be explained soon enough. You have come a long way to find me—and you are tired. Rest now."

Bryan was unable to resist the suggestion. Before his mind could formulate any words of protest, he was fast asleep.

Bryan felt a strong hand on his shoulder, but he wasn't startled. He looked up to see the old man standing by the fire. How could he have shaken Bryan from so far away? He suspected it was another trick for him to learn.

The man gazed at Bryan with deep, ageless eyes. "First, the term 'old man' will not do. My name is Lorne. You know there are monsters and demons in the world—and we have our grouping in them—but there are things in this world far more lethal. It is first necessary to tell you the story of us. You seem to have seen that you—we—are not as we appear."

"How old are we?"

"The only way to answer your question is to tell you the history of where you came from and what we are. In a time before written history, we were a noble people, nomadic, but proud. We lived and fought for our families and homes as did any other tribe scattered throughout Europe and Asia. We fought for land for hunting and farming, and we were driven away from those lands even as we drove others away. Such was the world in which we lived.

"As time went on, tribes grew or disappeared. Our tribe slowly faded from the world. We were a vanishing people. Eventually we began to build villages in areas rich in soil and resources. We fought many wars to keep these lands. As villages were destroyed, we became adept at making weapons and conducting war. We also learned many things about how to influence the outcome of each battle. We created a system of belief that was centered on the vital energy of our environment. This was the beginning of our religion, and it would shape our culture. In our development, we made many enemies—more than could be counted—and the storm that followed was the prelude to our being brought closer to the edge of destruction, and to what we are now.

"The priests who strengthened us learned to develop the abilities that would aid us in battle. The magic they harnessed—and the spells they created—would give us the strength of the bear or the cunning and savagery of the wolf at a time when these abilities were most needed. The priests called on the spirits of the forest to give us mastery of our weapons, and our rage, and superiority over our enemies, but the many years of war that followed cost too many warriors. Eventually our enemies drove us from our lands. We set out across the Carpathian Mountains with little to sustain us, and cold and starvation took as many as enemy arrows did.

"Finally, we found a land where we could rest, but as some knew we had to move on, others wanted to stay. The tribes in this new land were weaker than those we had fought years earlier, and some of our warriors were willing to fight to stay. They killed all who stood against them, and their lust for battle had taken hold, changed them. Our warriors wanted to establish kingdoms, and they obsessed about their new power. The priests refused to aid in this, and many of them were killed. Those who submitted were forced to pray to the gods, to call down the power for much more than battle. What was not known was that the priests called down the power of the gods to curse all those who fought to change them into terrible, distorted aberrations of the attributes they utilized in battle. Such was our beginning. The priests were hunted down and killed for their treachery, but one escaped, and he learned how to fashion weapons to destroy us. He warned others, trained them how to fashion and use these new weapons, and was killed soon after his escape.

"Many battles were fought, and it came to be that warriors of the bear form—berserkers they were called— were wiped out. The wolf survived only because of the cunning of the forest, and their brutal, savage nature to destroy all who stood before them.

"Terrible sickness struck, and many fell. We cursed the gods for what we had become, those who hunted man for food. We learned the cost of the curse we bore. Warriors, husbands, and sons could father no children. Wives would not survive to carry to childbirth. We also learned that a bite could change a man—or kill him. This was the price of our survival. A wife would have to be bitten, and if she survived the change, she would bear children. Even then, the birth was difficult, and the mother often died. Those who were bitten had the power to change as the moon changes, but they were weaker than those who were born to changed parents. Those born were called naturals, and they had a more powerful affinity with the forest around them, making them stronger, faster, and more cunning killers. Only naturals can resist the call of the moon, resist the bloodlust to hunt and kill.

"The secrets that were carried away by the priest were used to hunt us down, and we became children of the forest, never revealing ourselves to others. Many who were bitten were driven mad by the change, and they became the monsters that brought evil and death to those who traveled dark roads—or were foolish enough to hunt at night. Only those naturals who were strong enough to resist the taste of blood were allowed to carry the secrets of our beliefs. Of those, only the strongest would be chosen to become the master of the forest. The master is the one who must protect—and lead—with wisdom. Their task is to protect the secrets and keep the history from being lost. We exist only as stories to frighten children, but that is the price of our freedom. Those who hunt man must be stopped—or they will bring others to hunt us again."

"Do all shape-shifters find their way here?"

"No, a few find me, and they are the ones who help me protect the secrets. There are some who refuse to make the journey or are driven to kill before they understand what has happened to them, and they are who we fear."

Bryan saw everything with clarity. He felt like a child as he listened to every word. "When were you chosen to succeed your teacher?"

"Time matters little to me now, but if it helps you to know, it was a time when I came to the Americas. I followed the French here, helped them in their effort to liberate a fertile land from the English oppressors. Since then, I have seen many battles, but I have participated in none. We are as brutal and savage as we are secret, but the world of man has no equal in its measure of cruelty. Evil was brought to the world by the desires of man, and nothing can soothe the heart insatiably driven by lust for power."

The rational part of Bryan's mind thought the idea of such a long life impossible, but much of the cruelty displayed over countless years should have been equally impossible—and these facts could not be denied. It blurred the line between man and monster.

"We will start the teaching tomorrow. For now, it's time to rest."

Bryan was happy to see that Lorne lived in a small cabin like any other man of the mountains. He was glad to not have to find a comfortable spot in some dank hole.

CHAPTER 14

▼

Lyle had prepared a meal of venison, wild rice, and potato skins. Allen was glad to not have to cook—and Jason had the usual jokes about Allen's cooking—but they all agreed that Allen was a damn good cook.

"So what happens now?" Jason asked as he jabbed his fork into a large steak.

"We wait," Lyle said. "Bryan will figure out what to do. He'll get back to us in due time."

"Why do I sense there's something you're not telling us?" Allen asked.

"Because there is something I'm not telling you for your own good. You may learn the truth in time, but I hope not the way I anticipate."

"Now what the hell does that mean?" Jason asked.

"It means I think something is going to happen tonight or tomorrow," Lyle said. "I want you two to pack your things. Be ready to move at a moment's notice. We may have very little warning when it happens."

"What do you think is going to happen?" Jason asked.

"I don't know. What I do know is that you two are going back home at first light. I will be here when Bryan gets back."

"No, we came here—" Jason started.

"No!" Lyle shouted. "If this is going to work, you have to trust me. I want to make sure Bryan stays alive as much as you do, but this is something you can't help him with. The safest thing you can do is go home … or go into hiding. There is no other way."

Allen and Jason nodded in agreement and finished their meal in silence.

After the crockery was done, Allen and Jason got their packs together while Lyle brought out three rifles from storage.

"I haven't used these rifles in years, but I know that if the time should come, they will prove their value in a fight," Lyle said.

"Would you be willing to pass the time with a story?" Jason asked.

"Perhaps I—" Lyle started.

Allen and Jason stared into Lyle's ashen face.

"Lyle, what's wrong?" Jason asked.

Lyle didn't respond. A chill ran the length of his spine and settled in his brain.

"Lyle, what's going on?" Allen asked.

"Get your stuff together," he said as he reached for a rifle and loaded it.

"But—"

"Don't think. Do it now." Lyle ran to secure the door, and then he stepped to the side of the window. Allen and Jason grabbed the other rifles and loaded them. Lyle didn't think the cabin locks would do anything to keep this new threat from entering, but they would serve to announce from where the first attack would come. Lyle tossed Jason a set of keys. "When the time comes, you and Allen get to the truck. Drive like hell. Don't look back."

Jason opened his mouth, but he was cut off by the smash of the front window collapsing. They turned to face the enemy they thought was about to leap through the window. Instead, the front door was smashed in with terrible force, knocking Jason to the floor and causing him to lose his grip on his rifle.

Lyle turned and fired, but the shot was wide. The enemy spotted its first target, and it stepped toward Allen. Allen turned to fire, but he was grabbed and shaken, causing him to lose his rifle. Staring into a mouth of glistening yellow teeth, Allen raised his knees as hard as his muscles would allow and drove them into his attacker's midsection.

Jason regained his footing and swung his rifle as hard as he could. The barrel of the rifle rang out as it connected with the back of the monster's head. It grunted, lurched forward, and turned its hairy torso around to focus on Jason. Jason had no time to react. He tried to dodge whistling claws, but they slammed into his right side. Jason flew across the room and crashed into the bedroom door.

Allen saw an opening, drew his knife, and plunged it deep into the monster's left side. He was rewarded with a terrible scream of pain and anger. Allen was caught by the monster's claws around his neck.

As Jason tried for another attack, the monster parried the anticipated move and smashed him to the floor before it returned its attention to its helpless captive. Allen's neck was crushed with enough force to bend and shape cold steel. His lifeless body was hurled against the wall, resulting in another loud snap as he crumpled to the floor. The monster ripped the knife from its side, spraying blood across the walls as it threw the knife to the floor.

"Jason, run!" Lyle screamed.

Jason scrambled to his feet and jumped through the broken window, running as fast as he could for the truck.

The sound of the truck was enough of a distraction to give Lyle enough time to jump through the window. Once he was in the open, he could buy Jason the time he needed to escape. "Come on, you gruesome son of a bitch!"

The monster jumped through the window and headed for the truck, but Lyle was quick to block the path. Flying claws shot forward, but Lyle parried and sliced down hard, scoring a hit across the left shoulder as the arm was brought back. As soon as he heard the wheels of the truck spinning on gravel, Lyle feigned another attack. When the monster reacted, he turned and fled into the trees. After a hundred meters, he found the monster was not willing to give chase. He headed back to the cabin, staying in the shadows to avoid detection. He saw no sign of his attacker, but he saw his cabin aflame. He continued through the dark forest as the howling started. The howls of pain and frustration made Lyle smile as he ran. He knew Anton would think more carefully about his next attack, but Lyle would be ready the next time.

Jason and Lyle met in the hotel parking lot. Jason was fighting to maintain the little sanity he had; the only thing he knew for certain was that Allen was dead. The rest of the experience was lost in a haze. When he gathered his wits, he asked, "Lyle, what are we going to do now?"

"What are you talking about? We are not going to do anything. You are going home."

"What about Allen? Shouldn't we at least take care of him—go and bury him?"

"You're not going to find him. By now, his body has been moved."

"What the hell was that thing?" Jason did nothing to disguise the fear and pain in his voice. "It threw Allen like a tennis ball."

"Sit down," Lyle said. "I really hoped you wouldn't find out like this. There are things in this world that are almost impossible to explain. I think you know what that thing was, but I know *who* it was. I know he has not finished yet."

"Are you saying that he is coming after me next?"

"No. He'll come after you and me. He will not stop. All of us were his targets."

"How do I stop it?"

"You can't. I have to."

"Don't tell me that shit!" Jason barked. "If he is human, he can be killed. If there is a way to stop it, I want to know. And if you try to stop me, I will kill you."

"Are you finished? Think this through! You don't even know what you're dealing with—and you have no idea how to fight him. Nothing you do is going to fix this or bring Allen back. You saw what he can do. If you go into this unprepared, you'll be killed just as Allen was. Please, just trust me now."

"Okay … but I'm not going home."

"Why?"

"Because Bryan is still up there. And I made a promise that I would be here when he returned. Besides, if he is going to hear about Allen, he should hear it from me."

"There is nothing I can say to change your mind?"

Jason stared at Lyle. "Allen was my brother, just as Bryan is. Bryan is the reason we came back here. He deserves to know the truth. So what do we do?"

"Right now, nothing. It's too late to act. At first light, we'll go to the village to talk with Dario. He will know something, and I want some questions answered. Before we go back to the village, I need you to do something for me."

"If it involves finding an escape route out of town, you can forget it."

"No. I need you to go back to the bar and ask for my friend. Tell him what happened. He will gather some supplies and meet us at the village. Don't wait for him."

"Do you expect Mr. Ugly to come find us?"

"No, he'll be off somewhere licking his wounds. We should be safe for the night."

The night passed slowly, and neither man rested. It was difficult to sleep after the encounter. Jason could not push the terrible images out of his mind. He saw Allen's crumpled body, the terrible teeth, and the claws searching for another target. The screams of pain and fury echoed in his mind like an endless earthquake. He swore that he would see Allen's killer destroyed.

Jason looked out the window at the blackness and saw the first changes of welcoming violet. He sat in silence, trying to manage the phantom images that threatened to pull his sanity into the blind madness of panic.

"You didn't sleep at all, did you?" Lyle asked.

The question snapped Jason from his dark thoughts. "No, how could I sleep? How could I think about that when I know I'm being hunted? Oh yeah, I forgot to mention my brother is still out there somewhere, left to rot while we try to figure out our next move."

"All right! I get it. I'm sorry," Lyle said.

"I think I'm the one to apologize. None of this is your fault."

"No, but this is happening because of Bryan. When we get to the village, I need you to keep your temper in check. It will do us no good if you lose it—and the village is the last place for a confrontation."

"I just want the bastard who killed Allen."

"I mean it! No bullshit!"

Jason stared at Lyle for a moment. "I'll try."

"Thank you. Now please go find Henry. Tell him to have everything in place before he comes to the village."

"What does that mean?"

"He'll know."

Jason nodded and walked through the door. When he arrived at the darkened bar, Henry was the only one there. "Is this bar normally open so early?"

"This is a logger's bar. It never closes except on Sundays. What do you want?"

"Lyle sent me to find you." Jason explained the situation to Henry. When he explained Allen's death, it was difficult to keep his temper down, but he managed without getting too hot.

Henry nodded. "Tell Lyle I will be in the village in two hours."

"Okay, can you tell me—"

"No."

"But—"

"No! Go back and tell Lyle what I said. I will take care of the rest. While you're in the village, do yourself a favor and keep your mouth shut. Nothing you do or say will do anything to fix this. You're the lamb. Don't get killed because you got stupid and lost your temper." He walked out of the bar without waiting for Jason to respond.

Lyle was still in the room when Jason returned.

"He is on his way," Jason said.

"Good, get your things. We leave in ten minutes."

"Is he always so short-tempered?" Jason asked.

"Yes, but there is no one I trust more than Henry to do the task I have asked. He is the only man who knows this area better than me."

"I guess I'll have to settle with that. You guys are pissing me off with what you're not telling me. I still don't know what's going on. Is that guy a secret weapon or something?"

"Something like that … no more questions. We have to go."

Jason felt as though he had lost control of the situation. To be sidelined so easily made him feel like a feather in the wind.

Within minutes, they were on their way back up the mountain. On the gravel road, Jason noticed more dust than usual. Lyle pulled the truck to a hard stop in front of the village, dragging a huge brown cloud behind them. He waited for the dust to clear before opening his door. "Now remember, this is not the time or place to lose control of your senses," he said.

"Okay, let's get this over with," Jason said.

Lyle led the way to the main hall while Jason checked the area behind them. The village seemed unusually quiet, considering there was supposed to be a festival in a few days. Jason noticed a few people paying attention to them. Jason stayed on the front step while Lyle stepped inside to check the hall. "No one's here. We'll try Dario's office," Lyle said.

"Isn't this odd? There are only a few people here."

"Hush." Lyle's face reflected Jason's concern. "Dario never leaves his office locked unless there is a problem in the village. We'll try the clinic."

"Why?"

"Just a hunch. Allen's blade caused a wound that wouldn't heal up in twelve hours."

They heard voices near the clinic. Jason thought he heard Dario's voice with two others.

"Stay here," Lyle whispered as he walked through the front door.

Anton was standing behind a desk while a woman applied fresh bandages to his wound. Dario was behind the desk. All three heads turned to see Lyle and Jason standing in the doorway.

"I told you to stay put!" Lyle barked at Jason, and then he turned to face Dario. "You will call a meeting in thirty minutes. There are some things that need to be discussed."

"I will do nothing of the kind!" Dario growled. "Who the hell are you to tell me what to do here? And you brought him as well? That was a mistake."

"It is my right to request a meeting any time I damn well please. If you don't call a meeting, I will call the rangers and tell them smallpox hit this place. They'll come and burn this place to the ground. I think you and your slave have some things to answer for."

"Are you making an accusation?" Dario asked.

"Yes. You know what this is about. Jason, get the gasoline and flares out of the truck. I will be there in a minute."

Jason grinned. "With pleasure." He thought Lyle might be bluffing, but this action was enough to keep Dario off his guard. He stepped down the steps harder than necessary.

"Stop!" Dario shouted. "If you do this, you will die like no other has ever experienced. If you try to escape, I will hunt you no matter where you run."

"You can stop this. Call the meeting," Lyle said.

Dario's expression was cold and gray. He stared hard at Lyle. "Before long, you and I are going to have our time. And we will see who has the right to command the rest of the colony."

"I look forward to the day," Lyle said.

"You will have your meeting in thirty minutes. While I finish up here, go summon the rest of the council to the main hall."

The woman nodded and rushed from the room.

Lyle maintained his sights on Dario, but he was not going to drop his guard. He backed slowly out of the room, not releasing his sights until his feet touched the softer ground. He and Jason turned and started toward the main hall.

"That's playing a little dangerous, don't you think? I wasn't sure if that was a bluff or not."

"No, not a bluff. Take away his power base and he has nothing to hold on to, but that also makes him more ruthless and treacherous than ever," Lyle explained.

"Then why do it?"

"Because this exposes him. It makes him defenseless. If he doesn't stand to the challenge, he appears weak. Others would challenge him, and he wants to be the most powerful and the most unchallenged. Now he has to fight for what he has left, and he could face death from any of us if he does not overcome this challenge."

"I still don't understand how this helps us."

"You will. Just don't do anything foolish." Lyle stopped Jason at the front door. "You listen and don't talk. This is a meeting, not a fight. I will deal with this."

"Is Anton going to be here?"

"Yes, because he has to be."

Jason watched as others filed through the front door and assumed their appointed positions. He and Lyle were subjects of interest, and he wondered if that meant he was to be the main course. The two men followed the last of the audience inside, and then the doors were closed. They took two seats near the front of the room. The sun filled the room with light. Jason noticed Anton in a corner seat, but he hadn't seen him enter the room. Perhaps there was a rear entrance for security reasons.

Since Dario had to stand in defense, another member would have to chair the meeting. The other council members appeared put off by how the meeting had been called. Rumors rustled among the attendees.

Dario waited for the room to settle before addressing the council. Once the room was quiet, he said, "First, let me state that I did not call this meeting. I assume you have a damn good reason for bringing us all here." Lyle eyed Dario like a predator waiting to strike. "These men have something important to say—let them speak now."

Lyle stood and said, "I came here to address the council and to deal with an attack against me and my guest. I believe the attack was not brought before the council, and it was therefore not sanctioned, and the council has no knowledge of the incident. This attack has also resulted in the death of another, an innocent, who was also my guest."

"This is a serious accusation," Dario said. "Who are you accusing of this attack?"

"You." Lyle turned to Dario. "My cabin is burned to the ground, my guest is dead, and I stand here to accuse you and your puppet of murder. He wears the proof of this attack under those bandages." Lyle pointed to the wrapped wound Anton was trying to hide. Turbulent whispers flew through the room, and it took a moment for the room to settle down. "The attack happened about an hour after we addressed the council. It seems there is evidence of John's death that others do not want revealed. I think it's time to deal with this for what it is. I am prepared to call the rangers and have them investigate this for me."

There was another flurry of rumors and whispered suggestions, coupled with sidelong glances at both accuser and accused.

The chairman rapped his gavel to regain control, and slowly the room returned to a state of composure. "Do you have proof of this attack against John?"

"No, but John was beginning to link evidence in events at the same time as the arrival of my guests the first time they were on the mountain. He was killed to keep that evidence from being brought forward."

"If you had time, could you bring this evidence to the council?" the chairman asked.

"If I had time, yes," Lyle replied.

"Then I suggest—"

"Sit down and shut up!" Dario yelled.

"What is the meaning of this?" the chairman said.

"Shut up!" Dario yelled. He turned to Lyle. "You and your little whelp are no longer welcome here. John didn't have any new evidence, and the attack against you was not approved by me. If you have anything else to say, say it and get out."

"You have done enough to keep this situation hidden from the council," Lyle started. "You have two deaths to cover up, and more people will die before this is done. Your lies will not help you now."

Jason stood and was about to speak when Lyle pushed him back down.

Anton said, "You have gotten into my affairs for the last time. I should have killed you when I had the chance."

"Anton Bender, explain this to us," the chairman said.

"I was sent to kill another, but I would have killed them all if I had time."

"Then you admit to killing John?" Lyle said.

"Yes, but there are still three for me to kill," Anton said.

Dario slumped in his chair. This would be the catalyst that would destroy his power base. There was nothing he could do to stop it unless a miracle fell into his lap.

"Who sent you to kill the visitors?" the chairman asked.

"You know who … and you did nothing to stop me."

Lyle saw Jason was getting antsy; maybe it was time to let him speak. "Ask him why," he whispered.

"Why what?" Jason looked up.

"Why you and your friends were targeted."

"What good would that do? I don't care why he did it."

"Jason, you have the right to know."

"I don't care! I watched Allen die. That piece of shit killed my friend and I want to see him pay for that."

Anton stepped forward. "Look where you are, little man. There are no police here. I can do anything I want. I don't answer to anyone outside the village."

"You will answer to me! Why did you kill my friends?" Jason shouted. Lyle tried to calm Jason down, but he was pushed back.

"Because you are cattle!" Anton screamed. "Hell, your friend didn't even taste that good. Too bland for me, but I bet your blood would taste much better."

"You son of a bitch!" Jason said. "I will kill you the first chance I get."

"Oh, shit!" Lyle said.

"You are half right. I am a son of a bitch," Anton said. "But you will die the same as the others that I killed."

"Then let's finish this," Jason said. He shrugged Lyle's hand from his shoulder.

"Jason, no," Lyle said.

"Are you challenging me?" Anton said.

Dario watched the play with great interest. The hunger in his eyes grew as he hoped for the one thing that would be the solution to his problem.

"Yes," Jason said.

"Jason, you don't know what you're doing," Lyle said. He put his hand on Jason's shoulder to restrain him.

"Leave me alone," Jason said.

"Lyle, he has the right to challenge," the chairman said.

"But this is senseless," Lyle said. "You're going to allow this without the other crimes being answered for. He's going to get killed, and that's another body that will have to be covered up. How far does this have to go?"

"Anton has the right to refuse the challenge," the chairman said.

"No. I accept the challenge," Anton said.

"Then let me take his place. I will fight Anton," Lyle said.

"You know that's not how it works," the chairman said. "Once the challenge has been issued and accepted, it must go forward until one is left standing. Nothing can interfere with this—not even legal matters of a society you claim to support."

"But how can you just allow this? This cannot be the way," Lyle said.

The chairman rapped his gavel again. "No matter how this ends, the matter of your friend's death will be settled and there will be no investigation." The council nodded in support. Dario smiled at the opportunity. "All that remains is to set the time for the challenge."

Dario stood and said, "May I suggest that combat takes place two days from now—one day before the beginning of the festival?"

"Is that date acceptable to the combatants?" the chairman asked.

Anton and Jason stared at each other and nodded. Lyle wondered how he was going to tell Bryan what had taken place when he returned.

"Jason, I hope you realize what you've done," Lyle said.

"Yes, and you will tell Bryan when he comes back," Jason said without taking his eyes from his opponent.

"Then it is done. Two days from now, in the courtyard by the light of the fires, the combatants will meet, and their fight will be resolved."

"Then there is no other business," Dario said without giving Lyle any chance to add to the meeting. He walked out of the hall without being dismissed. The others took their cue and started out the double doors.

Lyle held Jason back until all the others were gone. "You realize you have just been maneuvered into committing suicide."

"What do you mean?" Jason asked.

"You have given Dario and Anton exactly what they wanted—a reason to kill you without the need to cover it up. No matter what investigation is done now, Anton will never be held accountable for this or anything that follows because of it. The proof I had against him is useless, and he is free."

"But you said you were going to call the rangers to have them tear this place apart."

"I can't do that now. Dario has an excuse to refuse them access to the village. That's what I was trying to tell you. Normal laws don't apply here—it's the same as a reservation run by proxy—and this was never about John or Allen. This has always been about Bryan." Lyle took a deep breath. "John found evidence on Dario and Anton that would have exposed them and their poaching, and the activities Dario has tried to keep secret from the council. This is not the first place bodies have turned up because of those two. John was supposed to bring me the information after he saw the old man, but he was tracked and killed before he got there. Now, I'll be lucky if I can find the information I need in six months. Between now and then, there's no telling how many more will die. It doesn't matter now anyway. Dario has control of the council."

Jason noticed Henry standing at the front of the hall.

"From the expression on your face, I'd say I'm too late," Henry said. "What happened?"

"Jason challenged Anton to a fight," Lyle said.

Henry immediately turned on Jason. "I told you to keep your mouth shut! You stupid ass! What the hell did you think you were doing?"

"Leave him alone, Henry. We have to prepare for the fight now."

"When is it going to be?" Henry asked.

"Two days from now," Lyle said.

"That means all the preparations I made are useless—not to mention that your guest has destroyed about six months of work," Henry said. "Have we given any thought to a plan B?"

"No, not yet," Lyle said. "Anton is still wearing the bandages. That means Allen's blade did more damage than any bullets would have. He has a weakness that can be used against him."

"Okay, let's get this worked out." Henry pointed at Jason as though he was addressing a disobedient child. "And you pay attention this time. When I say shut up, I mean exactly that. This time, do as you're told. With any luck, you might just survive the week … if I don't kill you first." They started out the door. "By now, Dario will have a plan set in motion. All we have to do is figure out what he's going to do."

"Why is that so important?" Jason asked.

"Because he is the one we are trying to destroy. Bryan was the one he was trying to stop," Henry said.

"I still don't get it," Jason said.

"The forest master has come back." Henry held his ground until Jason took a step back. "That was why Bryan had to see the old man."

"Enough, Henry." Lyle stepped between the men. "When we have time, I will explain it all to Jason."

***

The day of the fight was clear, and some preparations had already been made for the event. The fire in the central courtyard was lit even though dusk had not yet started. A small crowd was beginning to gather around the fire and there was much talk about the event to come—should either man survive. Dario and Anton had not yet arrived, but all the council members had arrived and taken their places among the crowd in anticipation of the main event.

As Jason, Lyle, and Henry walked across the courtyard, they were asked to take their proper places.

Lyle was going over strategy with Jason. "Remember, his size will make him difficult to topple. He has a longer reach than you so stay away from his hands if you can. He's going to favor his left side, so try to concentrate all your strike against that side to keep him off balance."

Dario and Anton had taken their places in the courtyard, and the combatants were directed to take their places. Jason waited for further instructions from the chairman. The ring was closed so that no one would be allowed to interfere. All present would make sure the ring remained unbroken. The combatants moved to opposite sides of the ring, staring hard at each other as they moved.

Silence hung heavy over the gathering. The darkening sky lent a surreal feeling to the event, and the fire burned in the courtyard. The full moon and stars glowed brightly as though the gods themselves were there to watch the show. Finally, with the sky near black, the chairman raised his hands.

"The fight is here; let it end here. Let the fight continue until one is left standing." He plunged a hunting knife into the earth a foot from the edge of the fire, and then he returned to his spot at the edge of the ring.

Jason eyed the knife, but he doubted he would have the chance to use it. Maybe he could make sure Anton wouldn't use it either.

The chairman raised his hand again, holding it high for one minute. The only sounds were the crackling fire and night creatures singing. "Begin," he said, and he lowered his hand.

Jason and Anton raced for the knife, but Jason dropped and rolled, forcing Anton off balance and struggling to maintain his footing. When Anton recovered, it was too late. Jason grabbed for the knife from his knees, and with all his might, he threw the deadly blade into the middle of the fire.

"Very clever," Anton hissed. "Now the odds are even."

The big man's strength came from his legs. Jason would have to be mindful that Anton was stronger and faster on the rebound. As they moved around the ring, Jason watched for an opportunity. He lunged for Anton's left side, forcing the big man to protect his rib. Jason dropped when Anton launched an attack. He drove his heel into the side of Anton's right knee, which cracked like a walnut shell.

The big man howled and fell to the ground. "God damn it!" He braced for the pain as he set the joint back in place, and he grunted as the joint crunched back into alignment.

"Now you got a handicap," Jason said.

"Think so? Bring it on then," Anton said.

Jason worked the same tactic again, but as he dropped, he shuffled to the other side. One hand landed squarely in Anton's groin, and the other crashed with terrific force into the soft spot on Anton's ribs. The reaction was immediate—as was the scream that followed. When Anton's left arm hit Jason's midsection, Jason flew ten feet through the air. He smiled through the pain as blood flowed through Anton's shirt.

Anton took a step back, and he felt the vital fluid oozing between his fingers. "You want a fight? All right, you little bastard."

Jason jumped to his feet and waited for the next attack. Anton was not holding anything back. Anton tried to dodge, but he was sent flying again. He looked around, but no one moved or cheered for one side or the other. Expectant faces hoped for the survival of one or the other. He knew he was in trouble, and it was time to get creative. Jason wiped the blood from the side of his mouth as he paced on the opposite side of the fire from Anton. Anton was motionless.

After a minute, Anton leaped easily over the fire and grabbed Jason by his lapels. Jason grabbed Anton by the shoulders, drove his knees into his solar plexus, and thrust his fist into the big man's throat. Anton staggered and fell to the ground. He quickly recovered his wits and kicked Jason's feet out from under him. Jason fell hard, but he was not stunned or damaged by the blow. Anton regained his feet and stomped forward. Jason grabbed a handful of burning embers and drove them into Anton's face. Burned and blind, Anton screamed as the coals seared through the skin on his face. As the embers fell onto Anton's shirt, burn marks and smoke began to rise. Jason reached into the fire for a burning log, and he swung as hard as he could. When it struck Anton, it set his shirt aflame. Anton thrashed and ripped off the burning cloak, flinging it out of the danger zone.

Jason still held his flaming weapon as Anton launched again. He swung again, but Anton caught Jason's arm and pulled down hard. The burning club was dropped as Anton repeatedly slammed a fist into Jason's side. Jason fought to wiggle free. He curled and brought his heavy boots into Anton's midsection, but this only served to make the big man lose control. Jason was thrown again, landing beside the fire. He fought and danced to get his shirt off before he was burned. As he stood, he saw the knife he had thrown into the fire. The beacon of hope was glowing like a patio lantern.

Anton stepped forward and raised a heavy foot to stomp on Jason's back. Jason summoned all his strength to reach the knife, and he rolled before the boot made contact. He swung the blade, slicing through Anton's calf. The big man screamed and fell, holding onto his severely damaged muscle. Jason rolled again and plunged the glowing dagger deep into Anton's belly. The big man screamed, and his pain and anguish echoed through the trees. Anton regained his feet, ripping the dagger out and throwing it to one side. He watched Jason struggle to raise himself, but Jason couldn't manage to get off his knees. Anton strolled over and grabbed Jason roughly, sinking his long teeth into Jason's shoulder. Jason no longer had the strength to voice his pain. After a moment, Anton released his victim and let him fall to the ground.

He turned to Lyle and said, "Now your cause is his—and you are next."

"You should have killed him," Lyle said.

Jason could only look on. As the last of his strength faded, he closed his eyes.

CHAPTER 15

▼

Richard Lee was startled awake by a loud knock at his hotel room door. He groaned and looked through bleary eyes at his wristwatch, which said 7:32. He hated flying, couldn't stand the jet lag, and—even though the flight to Fort Saint John was only two hours—he couldn't wait to be back on the ground as soon as the wheels left the tarmac. It felt like paying for a limousine but getting a rattletrap taxi.

"Hang on a sec," he called. A second knock urged him to the door. "I said hang on!" He forced himself to a stand long enough to don his robe and slippers.

Rick was surprised to see a smiling young officer at the door.

"Sir, my name is Constable Jensen. I was asked to meet with you to assist with your investigation."

Rick tried to close the door, but Jensen got a heavy boot in the doorframe before the door could be closed. The officer was tall and thin, but Rick could tell there was an unrevealed power that could prove as dangerous as it could be beneficial.

"When I spoke to your inspector, he said I should expect this from you this early in the morning. I'm sure our interaction would go smoother with a cup of coffee."

"How old are you?" Rick asked.

"I'm sorry, but what does that have to do with anything?" Jensen took off his service cap to reveal a short crop of blond hair. His fine features were hard to read in the subdued light. Rick opened the curtains, and the room was flooded with light.

"If I'm expected to work with a cub, I need to know what to expect if things get nasty."

"Richard, is it? Let me ask you something. What's the difference between the drug-choked scumbags you take down every day and the beer-slamming bullshit artists I have to deal with?" When Rick didn't answer, Jensen continued. "There is no difference. You took the same courses I did, fire the same weapons I do, understand the same principles I can, and have the same stupid attitude as everyone else. The poachers up here don't give a rat's ass what you look like—you can die like any other meat sack in a sweatshirt—and that makes them no different from your scumbags at home. I'm happy to help on any case where I don't have to play twenty questions to qualify for the position. So if you don't mind, I'm going to put on some coffee while you have your shower and wash the shit out of your head. Is that okay with you?"

Rick smiled and nodded, slightly amused by the rant. "That's fine. I won't be long." He hated fencing positions, especially when he felt the opposition was treading on sacred ground, but this young man handled himself well. He had set the record straight with Rick from the beginning and made it known that no bias would hold him back from doing his job. He liked this young man immediately—and thought he would do well in a firefight.

"By the way, you got a first name?" Rick called.

"Yes, sir. It's Francis."

"Francis?"

"Frank, if you prefer. It was my mother's choice."

"Frank it is then. Were you given any details about the investigation?"

"No. I was told you would brief me on my arrival here. It seems there is something peculiar the inspector thought you should tell me directly."

"Yes, but the details are rather grisly," Rick said.

Frank had poured two cups of coffee by the time Rick returned from the washroom. He took out his notebook and checked his notes. "I was told that a big man killed a good man and then ran here to the mountains. I think he was trying to have a sense of humor."

"Let's get something right. The inspector doesn't have a sense of humor. He has work he doesn't want to do. The good man that was killed had his heart ripped out of his chest—kind of like open heart surgery without the scalpel. His place was pretty busted up as well. Gave me the impression that it was more than a hate crime. This was personal, real messy."

"I've spent the last year going after poachers and such. When people cross the line with them, they don't just end up dead somewhere—they're left for the animals to clean up. I've seen bodies hanging from trees that had been there for a week before they were found. It leaves a hell of an impression when the only way to identify the bodies is to find the parts that have been buried or scattered over hundreds of yards. Poaching is big business in this part of the world, and there's no limit to the lethality these bastards will go to in order to protect their secrets."

"No shock and awe, huh?"

"Not one damn bit."

"Fair enough." Rick reached for a file in his carryall and handed it to Frank. "Here's the file. Familiarize yourself with the names. The crime scene is messy and confusing. Things don't get this bad unless there is something really big someone wants."

"I've seen this kind of thing before. It usually means something or someone has been exposed. It's meant to leave a message. If Bryan Delman did this, then he has no compunctions about killing again, given enough reason."

"Meaning what?"

"Meaning if this situation gets dicey, the only way you are going to stop your killer is by killing him. I don't think this was random. I don't think your killer will kill arbitrarily unless he is forced to do so. And I don't think he will stop until whatever mission he is on is complete."

"You make it all sound so cloak and dagger."

"Not at all. As I said, I have seen this before. When I go after poachers, occasionally I get a break and find one that doesn't want to do it anymore." Frank dropped the file on the bed. "There is always one who has seen too much and wants out. He's done wrong—and he knows it—but the simple fact is when you're in this business, you're in until you're dead. When poachers come to me, they don't stay alive very long. His partners eventually catch him, and the message goes out. When an innocent hunter gets caught up in it, this is the kind of scene you can expect. Someone took something of value to your killer. What was taken?"

"It was a business disc that would operate under all the exchange rates used by all the major trade corporations. It would have been worth millions over several years and could guarantee contracts that would offer the biggest returns on shipping and trading."

"I'm beginning to see the logic."

"You see why I want to find this guy? I think he was just a pawn in all this."

"Okay, so where do we start?"

"That's where you come in. I was told my guy came up here to do some moose hunting. You know this territory; you can show me the best areas for that."

"You won't find much here. You have to go out of town for that," Frank said.

"What about Pink Mountain?"

"Yeah, that's a possibility. There's been some poaching out there. Lots of hunters go there for moose. How do you know about that area?"

"It was mentioned. If I don't know where it is, maybe it would be a good place to hide."

"I read about a cabin burning down in that area. That's a good place to start. The drive is about three hours, but the hiking is a bit rough. We'll need to pack some stuff with us."

"Do you know anyone who could help us?" Rick did not like the idea of hiking in an unfamiliar area.

"No. There was a ranger in the area, but he hasn't been heard from in some time. It's believed he had an accident and was lost."

"How long has it been since anyone heard from him?"

"About a week, maybe more."

"Hmm. Timing is about right," Rick said.

"For what?"

"Who was the ranger in that area?"

"His name was John McCauley. He was about the best there was at catching poachers. With his experience, I don't—"

"Do you believe he got lost?"

Frank thought for a moment. "No. John was experienced; he knew the areas."

"What if he didn't have an accident? You said he was experienced. Can we contact someone at the ranger station?"

"I don't see why not. How soon can you be ready to travel?"

"In about five minutes."

CHAPTER 16

▼

For the first two days, Bryan did chores and menial labor, but he knew not to question the man who had assigned the tasks. The blisters on his hands were unbearable until he turned off the pain centers in his brain. He took little rest, and his meals were lighter than he was used to, but he didn't complain. Lorne was always watching Bryan work, but Bryan pretended not to notice.

Each day's work started before dawn. He did the smaller jobs until the sun was over the hills, and then he moved on to the more difficult work. He was plowing a small quadrant of field for crops that would be needed throughout the year. His tools were not modern, but he thought it was part of his training. After the field was plowed, he would need to repair the fences.

Around lunch, he stopped for a sip of water. His hands were caked in a mixture of dirt and blood. He saw the open sores—and the way his blood ran freely—and wondered why he didn't feel the pain anymore. Though his hands bled and his muscles ached, he forced himself to continue. When it became too dark to work, Bryan put away his tools and washed up for the evening meal. All meals were taken in silence; after dinner, Bryan would read aloud from a book Lorne had given him as part of his study. Lorne was always happy to answer any questions; it was part of the process.

After the fifth day, Bryan wondered about his friends and the village. Lorne would only say that they had their own battles to face, and then he pushed Bryan to continue his work. Bryan knew he was of no use to his friends until he had complete control of the worst part of himself. He knew it was all in preparation for his own battle.

On the sixth day, Lorne said, "Your work has done much to help us—much of it without my guidance. Take a step back and realize what you have gained in your short time here."

Bryan looked at his roughened hands. He felt a new strength in them; his arms had grown too. He had a realization that he could overcome any pain or discomfort. All thoughts of the outside world were lost in the sounds of the forest, and he walked as though his feet didn't touch the ground.

Lorne said, "Don't just feel the strength in your muscles; feel the air around you. You have done it before. You know how."

Bryan stopped and looked at Lorne. "You directed my dream. You were there."

"Yes, I was there as you expanded your senses in every way." Lorne pointed to a large rock beside a fallen tree that had become home to a family of raccoons. "Feel the rock, the cold rough surface. Feel the trees around you, and know that everything around you has substance you can see and touch. Even the people around you can be felt without being seen. This is one skill you can improve that will help to keep you alive."

Bryan listened as he expanded his awareness. Soon he could feel the rock as if he was standing beside it. He could feel his pores reacting as he felt every sharp edge, but he knew it was being done by limiting the concentration level of his mind so there would be no resistance.

"Good," Lorne said. "Keep your hands at your sides. You are not reaching for the rock. You are its reality, as real and unmoving as the mountain."

Bryan lowered his hands and took a deep breath. The rock became more perceptible. He could feel every crystal of its structure—even though the rational, chaotic part of his mind kept trying to distract him from believing what he was feeling.

"Push your hand into the rock."

The request seemed a bit odd, but Bryan pushed his hand mentally against the surface. The harder he pushed, the more the rock refused to yield.

"Remember, you have to get beyond feeling the rock in its accepted form of reality. Everything that exists in the accepted plane of reality also exists on another plane that can be accepted and is just as real. The essence of magic is to go beyond what is accepted or expected. When you can do that, you will see that there is no wall that can't be breached—and no boundary that can't be crossed." Lorne took Bryan's arm. "We'll try again tomorrow."

"It's hard for me to decipher what I'm feeling as real. I can feel the rock, but I can feel everything else around me at the same time."

"You have spent your life reacting strictly on a physical level—and every reaction could be measured."

"I don't understand," Bryan said.

"You love your brothers, and that is a fact that will not be questioned, but you are unable to physically illustrate your love for them. It is not something physical you can show me. You can't put it on a shelf and stare at it, and you can't hold it in your hands. It is simply accepted."

Bryan was beginning to see where this was going. "I guess it's because of what I feel, and what I feel goes beyond my ability to explain it."

"Okay, you know there is air around us. You can't see or smell or taste or hear it, and you can't feel it until you move. Without moving, prove to me that the air is real."

"I can't."

"Why not?"

"I don't have that ability. I have to accept that the air is as real as you."

"What makes it real?"

"I don't know. I guess I have to accept it on faith."

"Exactly. Just because something does not react to the characterizations of the senses does not make it less real. It is like the love you feel for your brothers; the idea is intangible, and you have accepted a faith that what you feel is real. This is the way many belief systems are explained. Magic depends on your ability to see and feel beyond what you know is real."

Bryan knew these ideas were dangerous because most people would resist them, preferring to live in misery and squalor because they knew it was real. Bryan was beginning to see all things as though he was looking through a dark curtain—looking at reality from backstage—to see all the things that could not otherwise be seen in the realms of the corporeal and the spiritual, the real and the ethereal. He felt as if the world had opened to its hidden secrets.

The next day started as any other, but Bryan had forgotten everything except the tasks he had set for himself. Lorne had other ideas.

"You will cut no firewood today—and your other chores will wait. I want you to find something for me."

Bryan dropped his tools and turned to face his teacher. "What am I looking for?" When he looked into Lorne's eyes, he could tell that no information would be revealed about the object of his search. He took a moment to catch his breath and gather his thoughts. When he closed his eyes, the only image that came to mind was the hunting knife. He tried to focus on another image, but his mind was focused on the knife.

"Don't concentrate. Allow your mind to see and feel the object that must be found. Focus on that."

Bryan nodded and took a deep breath. His mind came back to the image of the knife. As he followed where the image led him, he listened to the sounds of the forest until he reached the rock he had seen before. He listened as the air touched every blade of grass and every fluttering leaf. The image grew stronger until his mind stopped at the base of a large tree. As he rounded the tree, he found his knife—still sheathed and tied—on a large root. Bryan smiled and allowed his vision to return to normal.

"Well done. You are learning fast."

"Are you able to manipulate solid objects ... to move them?" Bryan asked.

"No. That would be altering the state of matter, and none of us has that power. This ability is only to see that which is hidden from your normal vision. If someone wants to keep something hidden, then finding your target will require more than this ability alone, and you are not ready for that. Now go get your knife. I will have dinner on the table when you get back."

No other chores were set for the day. While Bryan hiked in the direction his vision had led, he reflected on what he had learned. Without realizing how far or fast he was traveling, he found himself in front of the great tree. He found his knife and started back to the cabin. When he looked around, he didn't recognize any trail markers. He tried to focus on retracing his steps, but he saw nothing. He shifted focus to the cabin to allow his other senses to interpret everything around him. He could smell the soil where he had stepped, and he found his way back to the cabin. When the cabin came into view, he could smell the hot meal waiting for him.

"What took you so long?"

"I stopped to think for a moment."

"And got lost," Lorne said with a sidelong glance.

"I had a little trouble getting back, that's all."

Lorne saw no deception in Bryan's face. "Okay," he said.

Bryan ate his meal in silence, sensing his time there was close to its end.

CHAPTER 17

When Rick and Frank spoke to people in the village, Rick saw the tension. Questions were answered, but the looks were furtive. People seemed more evasive than normal, but Lyle's name did come up as a subject of interest.

"The people are scared," Rick said.

"Noticing that," Frank said.

Two men stepped out from a cabin, and one stepped forward to greet them. "Is there a problem, officers?"

Rick was immediately suspicious. "Who are you?"

"Name is Lyle Perry. I was informed of your coming."

"Then you are the one we were told to see. I am Richard Lee from Vancouver. This is my partner Frank Jensen." All men shared handshakes. "Is there someplace we can talk?"

"Of course, gentlemen." Lyle led them to the kitchen. "Would you like a cup of coffee?"

"After that dusty road, I think it's a good idea," Frank said.

"What can I do for you?" Lyle asked.

"First, you can stop pretending you don't know why we're here," Rick said. "If you were told we were coming, you know why we're here."

Lyle chuckled. "I'm sorry. I do know, but I think my limited knowledge will be of little use to you. I have a case of my own."

"And what case would that be?" Frank asked.

"As I'm sure you know, John McCauley is normally here to oversee investigations in this area, but he was killed a short time ago. I have been looking into this to determine what happened to him. It's possible he was murdered."

"Why hasn't this been reported through proper channels? I've heard nothing of this," Frank said.

"Because of the poaching ring we've been trying to break for almost a year now. It's possible that John found something that got him killed. Bringing this to light would have destroyed any chance we had to stop the poaching or find the truth about John. I'm sure you understand the importance of not exposing those who are under extreme pressure to stop this kind of criminal activity. I need to be sure before I can present evidence."

"Okay, please tell us what you know about Bryan Delman. We were told you had contact with him recently."

"Yes, I did. He and his friends were here at a festival, but I couldn't say where Bryan is now."

"When was the last time you saw him?" Frank asked.

"It's been at least a week. I heard he went up the mountain alone. He could be anywhere up there. The man I have going after him should be able to find him though."

"Isn't that a bit odd? Bryan's from the city. What experience could he have to navigate this territory?" Frank asked.

"I was told he had been in this area before, but I don't know when. I have no idea what experience he may have," Lyle said.

"When do you expect your man back?" Rick asked.

"In about three days. If he hasn't found signs of Bryan by then, he probably won't."

"What about his friends? Do you know where they might be?"

"I know of one. Would you like to see him?"

"Yes, if that's possible."

"Follow me." Lyle led them to the cabin where Jason was unconscious. His scars and bruises stood out like neon signs.

"How long has he been like this?" Rick asked.

"Four days. He was near death when I found him. I've been keeping him safe since then."

"What happened?" Frank asked.

"He couldn't talk when I found him. From the way he's busted up, maybe he found something he shouldn't have. It's more common than you know out here. That may be why Bryan disappeared."

"Shouldn't he be transferred to a medical facility?" Rick asked.

"If you want to kill him. He's not going anywhere for a while. He won't be well enough to travel for at least a few more days. It's difficult to get anything up here to do an airlift unless it's an emergency. Besides, I have all the medical supplies I need to care for him. There's nothing else we can do for him right now." Lyle escorted the officers from the cabin.

"If you think of anything else," Frank said.

"Of course. I had hoped to be of more help, but I'm the only authority in this area until the government sends me another ranger. If you find anything that will help my investigation, I would be most happy to share the information with you." Lyle shook hands with the officers. "I hope you'll be staying in town for a bit."

"Did that seem a bit too smooth to you?" Rick asked as he climbed back into the truck.

"It did a bit, but I believe he told us what he could," Frank said. "He's holding something back, but I understand the need for him to do so."

"Fair enough, but I'm still not convinced that he told us the truth. There's more that we haven't been told."

"If what he is telling us is accurate, he may not be able to tell us more. I'm curious, but what can we do?"

"You heard him; he's the only authority in the area. Maybe we can dig up some dirt, see what's going on. There's nothing else for us to do."

"What did you have in mind?"

"I want to make some calls to see if I can get the okay to open some old files. Then I—"

Rick was cut off by a loud bang, and the steering wheel jerked hard left in Frank's hands. Frank struggled with all his might to keep the truck from going over the edge. He regained control and stopped the truck in the middle of the road. A cloud of dirt allowed no vision beyond the glass windows of the truck. They waited for the dust to clear before getting out.

"What the hell just happened?" Frank asked.

Rick walked around the truck and pointed to a rear tire. "This," he said. He stood with his hands on his hips.

Frank walked around and looked at the tire. The bullet hole was unmistakable.

"Son of a bitch, somebody shot out the damn tire!"

"I can see that. Thank you," Rick grumbled. "It seems someone has taken an interest in our investigation."

"Someone who could take another shot if he wanted to."

"I don't think so. Listen."

"What? I don't hear anything," Frank said.

"That's my point." The wind moved through the high branches of the trees, but nothing else stirred to give away their presence. "If someone wanted us dead, we would be dead now. There's no way to track where the shot came from."

"We'll never find anyone in this thick brush. Whoever shot the tire did what he meant to." Frank looked at the afternoon sky. "From where we are now, it would take roughly two hours to hike back to the hotel. The day is going to be hot, and we didn't bring enough water. We can change the tire and hope our sniper doesn't shoot out the spare." Frank started to get the equipment from the back of the truck.

"What happens then?"

"Then you have a choice to make. Either we hike back to the hotel or we drive on the rims to the nearest gas station to get the tires replaced. We can't stay here; nothing is safe out here after dark."

Rick moved to the back of the truck. "We better get started then."

Eventually they were moving again, but the spare tire was rough and the ride anything but comfortable. They rode in silence and waited for the next shot that would cause them more delays, but no shot came. When they got to the blacktop, the rest of the drive was free of trouble.

At the hotel restaurant, they picked up menus, but they weren't hungry. They picked a corner table so they wouldn't be noticed. "First thing in the morning, I'll make some calls to see what's going on. Did you want to make a trip up to the ranger station?" Frank asked.

"No, my interest is Bryan Delman. I'd like to know what happened to his friend. We know Bryan was on the mountain, but we don't know where. I don't want to waste more time trying to find him when I have no idea where to look." Rick sipped his coffee as the waitress took their order. "You notice we're being watched?" Rick whispered. He tried to focus on nothing as he took in his surroundings.

"Yeah, big guy in the corner. I saw him in the village moving stuff around, but it looked like he was hurt too."

"You recognize him?"

"Nope, never saw him before today. You want me to see what I can find on him?"

"It's coincidental, but it makes me nervous when someone is so obvious in his observations. Maybe I'll take a trip to the ranger station to poke my nose around." Rick sipped his coffee, trying to appear casual. "I'll bet if there is poaching in the area, the files on it will be there, and his picture will be somewhere in those files."

The dark figure made no effort to hide his interest in the officers.

"Then what?" Frank asked as he picked at his meal.

"Then I want to go back and ask Lyle Perry some more questions."

"Okay, and I'll go—"

"No, I need you to follow him, see where he goes."

"Are you sure that's a good idea?" Frank asked.

"Not entirely. Poaching is like drugs back home. The game is the same, and people still get killed. Be careful." Rick watched the big man walk out of the restaurant and around the corner. "You want a chance to impress me? Now's the time."

"Okay, I'll call you in an hour."

"Call me every hour, and get out of that uniform."

"You got it." When Frank got to the parking lot, the large man was gone. "Jesus Christ in a swimsuit!" He checked all the vehicles and around the building, but there was no trail.

Rick joined him a moment later. "Problem?"

"There's no sign of our guy. All the cars are the same as when we arrived, and there are no tracks. He just disappeared like a bad rumor."

"What do you mean?"

"I mean he's gone! I can't find anything that shows he was even here. The tree line is seventy yards away. How the hell can anybody close that distance so fast?"

Rick looked at the trees. "You'd have to be part greyhound to do that."

"I got a good look at him. He wouldn't be hard to spot in a crowd."

"I'm going to get changed," Rick said. "Now that everyone in town knows who we are and why we're here, there's no point in showing the uniform off."

They walked to their rooms, unaware of the watchful eyes above them.

Rick and Frank enjoyed a late meal as they discussed what they had learned from their adventure, and they worked out a plan for the morning. It was pitch black by the time Frank said goodnight and started off to his room. As he stepped into the night, he inhaled deeply, enjoying the smell of the trees. The night seemed untroubled as he listened to the light breeze moving through the trees and the insects in chorus. He was about to start up the stairs to his room when a quick movement caught his attention. He turned in the direction of the movement, but he saw nothing but cars in the distance. He walked to the corner of the building, but there was no trace of anyone. Satisfied with his brief scan, he started up to his room.

He was about to insert his key when he heard claws on wood. He looked around but saw no activity. He put his key back in his pocket and stepped cautiously down from the landing, trying to determine the source of the sound. There was no sound coming from any of the doors and no sign of life in the parking lot. The night was utterly silent. He stopped at the first step, but there was still no sound from the third floor or under the deck.

Frank felt at his side and realized he had left his sidearm in his room. As the regret and anguish of this mistake sank in, he turned and trotted quickly back to his room. He pulled the key from his pocket when he heard a loud thump on the landing. A large figure with powerful arms and large teeth stepped forward. "Holy shit!" Frank kicked the door with all his strength as the beast jumped forward. The door exploded inward as sharp claws surrounded Frank's throat and hauled him back. As the door swung back, the beast jumped again. Within seconds, it had reached the safety of the trees. Lights came on in the next room. An old man poked his head out his door, but he saw nothing of interest. He went back inside and turned out the lights. The night was still and silent. After a while, the insects started their chorus, and the night returned to its regular rhythm.

Rick had been so tired that he had not noticed the noise around the hotel. When he woke, he felt ready to take on the day's challenges. He dressed quickly and gathered his gear, feeling energized. As soon as he saw Frank's door ajar, he was scared. Wood and metal were strewn all over the floor. He raised his pistol and stepped cautiously into the room.

"Frank?" he called. He saw Frank's service pistol on the nightstand. There was no activity, but he did see claw marks on the wooden handrail. They were deeper than could be made by a dog or wolf; Rick thought a bear must have made them. When he saw spots of blood on the floor, he took out his cell phone and dialed the authorities.

It took an hour for the officers to arrive.

"Officer Lee? I'm Sheriff Cyril Abbott. That's my partner, Antony Hawes. Can you tell us anything?"

"I was coming down to wake my partner and found his door busted open. I checked inside, but the blood and the marks on the handrail were all I could find."

"Okay, who's your partner?"

"Frank Jensen."

"I know him. Can you tell me what you were working on?"

"He was helping me get to know the area. I came here to find someone suspected of a killing in Vancouver. He was working a case involving some killing up here. His case was a matter of tracking poachers. Now it seems these cases are connected."

"Perhaps someone has taken a personal interest in both your cases. If these cases weren't connected before, they are now. There's nothing more for you to do here. I'll tear this place apart to find anything I can. As soon as I have something, I'll call you."

"Thank you. If you don't mind, I have to make a trip up to the ranger station. I was wondering if you had a map I could use."

"You might want to stop at the hospital. There's someone you should talk to."

"Who?"

"There's a woman there who worked at the ranger station—until something happened. My partner can set you up."

Rick followed Anthony to the truck and was handed a map.

"Just follow the old trading post road," Anthony said. "About halfway up, you'll see a side road pointing up to the observation tower. The left road will get you to the station."

"Thank you."

The first stop was the trauma ward to see the girl. The front desk registered him as a visitor because she was closely guarded as a witness. Her doctor was not available, but a nurse directed Rick to her room. A guard waited for him to present the proper identification.

"How is she?" he asked.

"She's in pretty rough shape. She was beaten so bad, she was unrecognizable, and then she was left to the animals. A hunter found her and brought her here."

Her eyes were swollen shut, and her skin showed rainbow hues from the bruising. Her arms and legs were in casts to keep her limbs immobile. Hospital blankets covered the rest of her body. Seeing that she was unconscious, he walked and sat in a chair. As soon as a doctor entered the room, Rick pulled out his wallet.

"What are you doing here?" the doctor asked. He leaned forward to examine the presented identification. "You're a little bit out of town, aren't you, Officer Lee?"

"I'm investigating a murder back home that has led me here. Your patient may be involved."

"Well, you won't get anything out of her," the doctor said as he motioned Rick to the door. Out in the hall, the doctor continued. "She's been like this for days. When she was brought here, she said, 'Dario was sent here.' She slipped into unconsciousness and hasn't come out of it since. I don't expect her to survive."

"How bad is she?"

"Almost all of her ribs were broken, as were both arms and legs. Some of the bones were shattered, and many of her muscles have been badly crushed. She has several bite marks on her body, and some of them look human. This was done to make her suffer the greatest agony before she dies. I'm no specialist in the field, but I'd say she crossed the line with the wrong person. This must have been a message for anyone who followed her."

Rick followed the directions to the ranger station. After an hour, he found the fork in the road. The road was as pitted as the road past the trading post.

Rick drove until he came to a large pile of blackened boards and charcoal. It was the only evidence that a building had ever been there. He took a deep breath and stepped out of the truck. There were spots of smoldering ash, and thin fingers of smoke rose from the ruins. He knew the fire had been set deliberately. *This is really beginning to piss me off,* he thought as he climbed back into the truck.

Back in the parking lot, Rick checked his firearm. As soon as he stepped out of the truck, he felt the heat of the day. The sun threatened to cook anything that wasn't moving. This made him more irritable as he started toward Jason's cabin. Halfway up the trail, Dario and many villagers intercepted him.

"Where's Lyle Perry?"

"He's busy," Dario said.

As the crowd moved in, Rick backed away from the cabin, raising his pistol.

Dario raised his hand, and the crowd obeyed the unspoken order. "You won't need your weapon. No one will attack you unless I give the word."

Anton stepped forward to stand beside his master.

"What's going on?" Rick demanded. Escape was no longer an option. He saw people around the truck, and he knew the only way out was shooting. "What the hell are you doing?"

"I have no doubt you know what happened at the ranger station," Dario said. "That is what led you here. You should know there will be no reinforcements to come to your rescue. You and your partner have learned far too much. And we would be honored if you would join us on a more permanent basis."

Some of the villagers appeared to change subtly. Some sported beards where there were none before.

"What the hell are you talking about? Where is my partner?"

"He's safe. He's here," Dario said.

Lyle stepped out of the cabin. As soon as he saw Rick, his expression changed to one of chagrin. "Officer Lee, I'm sorry you had to find your answers like this. I was disappointed to find out your partner had been abducted."

The tension in the air exploded like a volcano as soon as Dario and Lyle faced each other.

"This is not your show," Dario growled

"You will not hurt this man!" Lyle shouted. There was a separation in the crowd as camps were chosen amid a crescendo of growls and snarls of anger.

Dario waited for the guttural music to diminish before speaking. "The officer will not be harmed. He will join his partner as my personal guest."

"Your guest," Lyle sneered. "You are willing to resort to murder and abduction to have your show. You have abused your power and your hospitality, and people have died. You will not hurt this man or any other." Lyle restrained himself from allowing the rage to take hold. He stayed at the cabin door as the drama played out.

"As you wish," Dario growled. He pointed to a far cabin. "Your partner is there."

Rick didn't lower his pistol as he moved through the crowd to the cabin. He watched the crowd with the eyes of a madman about to be hanged. The crowd granted him access while maintaining a close distance around him. Rick felt as though he was walking a gauntlet that could turn on him at any moment. Frank was on a bed with a thick bandage around his neck.

"Frank, you okay?"

Frank nodded and pointed to his throat. After a moment, Lyle joined the two men.

"Lyle, what the hell is going on here?" Rick asked.

"I'm sure your friend could give you answers—if he could talk through the claw marks on his neck."

Frank made clawing gestures with his hands and pointed to his teeth.

"Christ, this isn't real. This can't be real," Rick said.

"It's as real as the forest around you," Lyle said. "Contrary to the popular myth, we are real, and we have a long history. Most people tend to believe whatever illusions they want in order to suspend their fear of the things that walk the dark shadows of the night. Their illusions and disbelief protect us."

Rick sat on the bed next to his partner. He wondered if there would be anyone to tell this story to. "My friend," he said. "I think we have gotten ourselves into a situation well beyond our control."

Frank looked at Rick as if to say, "It wasn't your fault."

Rick wore a plastic smile as he looked at Lyle. "I guess the only thing for us to do now is wait and see if your friend turns up."

Chapter 18

▼

Morning fog hung on the ground like spider silk on the grass. The bright sun promised a hot, sticky day—with no breeze to ease the discomfort. Bryan was concentrating on tying two logs together to repair a section of fence that had collapsed when Henry approached from the tree line. As he passed, Henry nodded his greeting and went on to the cabin. Bryan continued with his work, knowing he would be called if the situation required. Within seconds, he felt a strong urge to return to the cabin.

When Bryan arrived at the cabin, he was urged to a chair. Henry was sweating and needed a moment to recharge his strength.

"It's time for you to return to the village," Lorne said.

Bryan felt a stab of worry. "What happened?"

Lorne nodded his approval.

Henry said, "There's been some trouble at the village. Lyle sent me to get you back as quick as I could. He will explain the rest when we get there."

"But my studies—"

"They will wait," Lorne said. "We have no more time. It's time for you to use what you know to assume your place. You will not understand this, but I will not be here when you get back. And all I have left here belongs to you now."

"What do you mean?"

"As with all living things, the circle must continue, and all things must find their place within it. You have to find your place without me. Get your things. I will help you pack for the journey."

Bryan was confused, but he obeyed. Within minutes, he and Henry were back on the trail. Henry was puffing harder than normal, but he was keeping pace.

"Are you okay to make the return trip?" Bryan asked.

"We may have to rest in a bit, but I'll be fine. It's more important for you to get back to the village than for you to care for me."

"Can you tell me anything?"

"No, that is for Lyle to explain. We must hurry."

They pushed on despite the heat. After a while, Henry was gasping and nearing the point of collapse.

"Okay, we're stopping now. You need to rest." Bryan sipped from a canteen and handed it to Henry. Henry took the canteen but didn't drink.

"We don't have time for this."

"Drink," Bryan ordered. He watched closely to make sure Henry didn't lose control of his senses. He noticed something different about the way he smelled. "You're not a changeling, are you?"

"No, but I know the mountain better than any of my people."

"And your brother."

Henry's eyes went wide.

"Yeah, I know about Lyle. No one else will." Bryan picked up his pack and helped Henry with his. On the way down the trail, they were careful not to waste too much energy. He set a slower pace so Henry wouldn't be faced with complete exhaustion before they set camp. At dusk, they found a rocky outcropping that was secure from the elements. They didn't light a fire so there would be no sign for anyone watching. They would be back on the trail in less than six hours. With luck, they would be back in the village four hours after that. Bryan slept lightly—more concerned with Henry's safety than with recharging for the rest of the hike.

When morning came, Henry had a fever.

"You go no further. I'll make the rest of the hike alone."

"I need time to rest. I'll be fine."

"No, you won't. You pushed yourself too hard." Bryan handed Henry his canteen. "You take the water. Drink it all."

"You need water too."

"I'm not sick. You go home and get some rest. I will take care of everything when I get back to the village."

Bryan hiked for six hours without stopping to rest. When he reached the edge of the village, there was far more activity than usual. Bryan hid his pack in a hole, strapped his knife to his ankle, and started down to the fire pit. When Bryan saw Lyle moving between cabins, he decided to follow him.

When Bryan saw Jason's injuries, his anger immediately reached a fever pitch.

"I will explain everything," Lyle said. He took Bryan's arm and led him outside. He told Bryan everything.

"Jason doesn't know yet. His body has been fighting the infection, but it's only a matter of time."

"Is he well enough to travel?"

"Not yet—but he will be in a couple of days. He needs rest," Lyle said.

"There's no time for that anymore." Bryan turned and headed for the office.

"What are you going to do?"

"I'm going to find the bastard responsible for this mess."

Bryan found Dario in the courtyard with a crowd around him. The two officers, as Dario's guests, took their places behind him.

"Welcome home, Bryan. I imagine you have some questions for me."

"No longer," Bryan said. "Murder, kidnapping, extortion—I have my answers." Bryan watched as the crowd separated into two groups. From behind Dario, he watched Jason join his friend with some assistance from Lyle. Bryan spied Anton, and time stopped as his anger flared. "You killed Allen."

"And took him." Anton pointed to Jason.

"You should have killed him." Bryan looked at the officer with the bandage on his throat. "You take him too?"

"No," Dario interjected. "He was brought here as my guest."

Bryan looked at Dario, and he finally saw the connection. He saw the history of the village, and he knew it was one more battle in the war that was still to be fought. "You were going to kill all who came in contact with this village unless they were bitten. You killed my father."

"The secret of this place has to be protected, Bryan."

"You lied to me. You should have killed me when you had the chance."

"You know what to do. Kill me and take my place."

"I don't want your place. I want your head!" Bryan growled. As soon as he stepped forward, Anton moved to intercept, but Bryan allowed his anger to fuel his rage. Anton moved to strike, but Bryan moved with blinding speed and easily avoided the heavy fist. He sidestepped and wrapped his hands around Anton's throat. With one quick motion, he tore out the larynx. Bryan moved again and severed the carotid artery behind the left ear. Anton's body fell to the ground. "You have no champion. I will fight you tonight—and you will not see another dawn."

"As you wish," Dario replied.

The crowd formed a circle as the two men assumed their places in the field of combat. When twilight settled, the campfires were lit. Hours passed, but neither man moved nor spoke. Soon only the faces around the fire were recognizable by the light of the fire. The full moon was surrounded by a faint halo of stars shining like diamonds. The moonlight did nothing to hold back the shadows. It was as though a blanket of darkness had been cast over the area. No wind blew, and the forest made no sound. Only the sound of the crackling fire was heard.

When the sky turned black, Bryan removed his shirt, changing as he did so. Dario did the same, revealing terrible scars from previous battles. After several minutes of posturing, the men crashed together in a mad clash of snarls and blows. Dario punched hard, and Bryan fell back. Bryan stood up, and they came together again, exchanging blows. Dario raked his claws across Bryan's chest. Bryan howled and fell to his knees, sinking his own claws deep into Dario's belly. Dario jumped back in pain, and Bryan's chest bled freely as he regained his feet.

Dario grabbed a burning log from the fire and swung hard. It caught Bryan across the face. Bryan screamed as he wiped the embers from his eyes and tried to regain his senses. Dario swung again, but Bryan was able to duck. He slashed across Dario's chest and right arm, forcing him to drop the flaming baton. Bryan moved as quickly as he could to take advantage of the opening, kicking with all his might into Dario's solar plexus. Dario's strength was enough to keep him on his feet, but the blow nearly knocked him into the fire.

They launched again, colliding with terrible force. Dario brought a heavy fist down across Bryan's shoulder, knocking him to the ground. Bryan used the momentum, and grabbing a wrist as he went down, pulled hard. Dario went down in a heap, but Bryan had lost precious time. Dario was on his feet faster than Bryan could recover, and his boot crashed down on Bryan's back, smashing him to the ground. Dario stepped forward to kick Bryan, but Bryan caught the boot and rolled as he twisted, bringing Dario back to the ground.

Dario was first to his feet. His claws found their way around Bryan's throat. Bryan could feel the air being squeezed out of him as claws sank deep into his flesh. Bryan tried to reach for his knife without giving Dario more leverage. Bryan's strength was slowly draining away. With a great burst of strength, Bryan kneeled hard and pulled with all his strength. Dario tumbled and lost his grip, rolling over his enemy. He rolled too far to recover, and Bryan whirled and ripped his knife from his ankle sheath. When Dario saw the knife, he jumped over the crowd, running for the safety of the trees. Bryan grabbed a burning log and threw it through the window of what had been the office.

"What are you doing, Bryan?" Lyle asked.

The crowd watched in horror as the building was quickly engulfed in flames.

"Lyle, set the rest of the village on fire," Bryan said. He turned to the others. "This village was built on corruption and lies. It ends tonight." He turned and ran for the darkness, following Dario's trail.

Bryan followed the trail for an hour, finally coming to the rocky area he had seen earlier. The trees were smaller, and the trail was harder to follow. There were plenty of hiding places, but there was nowhere to run. He knew Dario was trapped, but he was surprised to see Dario waiting for him on the other side of the rocky minefield. He carried nothing that Bryan could see, but assuming his enemy was unarmed might prove a fatal mistake. As he moved closer, Bryan could smell the pungent stink of fear.

"You are quick to figure out where I'd run," Dario said.

"You stink," Bryan said. The only thing he smelled was the rank smell of his enemy.

"You are my destroyer. Should I not fear?"

"Won't do you any good. You know why I am here."

"You can have the village. I will leave—and you will be leader."

"Not enough."

"Why?"

"I would be a fool to think you have any good left in you. This ends now."

"Then let us finish it." Dario slapped his hands together. In a flash of light and a clap of thunder, he disappeared.

Bryan was momentarily stunned, but he recovered his senses quickly. He dropped to a knee and sniffed the air, but there was no longer a smell to detect. He focused on the ground, but there were no tracks to follow. Dario was using the rocks as his pathway. As he poked his head around, he felt a blow on his temple. He picked up the rock that had hit him, and he smelled his own blood. Shaking the pain from his head, he heard the footsteps of his enemy.

Bryan knelt again and started talking in a language that had not been used for hundreds of years. His senses changed, and he saw footsteps. His new vision allowed him to see the vital energy of everything around him; even though the vision lacked color, it was far more detailed. He saw the aura of everything organic and inanimate, and he saw where the aura had been disrupted. His enemy was thirty yards away, waiting for another opportunity to strike. When the attack did come, Bryan was able to easily avoid the missile. Bryan launched, colliding with Dario, and raked his claws across Dario's chest.

Dario whipped around and slashed Bryan's belly, but the wound was not serious. The fight became blade against blade. Bryan knew Dario's blade was not magical because if it was, Bryan would have already died when it cut across his fingers. Dario raised himself and lunged again, pinning Bryan against a rock with Dario's blade at his throat. Bryan forced Dario's arm back far enough to sink his teeth in it and forced Dario to drop his knife. Dario howled and slashed his claws across Bryan's face, forcing him to drop his own knife.

The combatants wrestled and slammed each other from rock to rock. As Bryan was beginning to tire, they tumbled into a steep ravine. At the bottom, they recovered slowly. When they found each other, they continued the struggle. Dario finally broke free of Bryan's grasp and ran for cover in the trees.

Bryan steadied himself and mustered all he had left to chase Dario into the darkness. Since he knew Dario would try for an easy kill, he moved cautiously through the trees. Several minutes passed without a sign of Dario. Bryan started up the hill to retrieve his knife, but he was blindsided when Dario launched at him with Bryan's blade. Bryan fell hard, but he saw an opportunity and pushed his claws into Dario's throat. Dario screamed as Bryan ripped the knife from Dario's grasp and pushed the knife edge at his throat. In exhaustion, Dario let his hands fall to his sides.

"It makes no difference now," Dario said. "Marco will kill everyone around you and leave you to your misery."

Bryan pulled Dario up, still holding the knife, and stared at his enemy. He pushed the knife slowly into Dario's throat, feeling Dario struggle as the last of his life left him.

"For Allen," he said. He let go of the knife and forced his claws into Dario's chest and gripped his heart. He ripped his hand free to show Dario the heart that beat twice before stopping. He let Dario's body fall, spoke a few words, and set the body on fire. There would be no grave marker.

Bryan staggered back into the village and held out Dario's heart for the crowd to see. He threw the heart into the fire. Lyle and Jason came to his side.

"Now it's over," Bryan said.

"What do we do now, Bryan?" Lyle asked.

"We move to another area. No one can know we were ever here. Lyle, can you cover this up?"

Lyle nodded. "I'll need Jason to come with me. He can never leave now."

"What about home?" Rick Lee asked.

Bryan faced the officer. "I'm sorry that Brent is dead, but you know I can't go back with you—and neither can Jason. Go back and tell them that Bryan Delman died in this fire."

Bryan walked through the thick smoke into the blackness. The crowd watched him until the smoke hid all there was … and Bryan was gone.